CHESSBOXER

CHESSBOXER

STEPHEN DAVIES

ANDERSEN PRESS

First published in 2019 by
Andersen Press Limited
20 Vauxhall Bridge Road
London SW1V 2SA
www.andersenpress.co.uk

2 4 6 8 10 9 7 5 3 1

British Library Cataloguing in Publication Data available.

ISBN 978 1 78344 840 1

Printed and bound in Great Britain by Clays Ltd, Elcograf S.p.A.

Play the opening like a book
Play the middlegame like a magician
Play the endgame like a machine

Rudolf Spielmann, grandmaster

PART ONE: OPENING

*A single exposure to chess is enough to make an
addict of anyone with a sense of adventure*

Edward Lasker (1885–1981)

My name is Leah – aka Chessgirl – and this is my first post. I'm blogging for me, not for you, so if you don't like what I write, just move on. You won't be missed.

My life is a moldy cake with five ingredients.

1.   Playing chess
2.   Staying in hotels
3.   Getting yelled at by Mom
4.   Getting yelled at by Coach
5.   Running, swimming, skipping and shadow-boxing

I'm in India at the moment, not that I've seen much of it. I'm cooped up in a hotel, playing at the Pune Open Tournament. By the end of Day Two I've got three wins from three games and Coach starts saying I have a good chance of winning the whole thing.

Day Three, and I'm up against an old Belgian grandmaster with the biggest forehead I've ever seen. I'm not kidding, it's big enough for four people. I open on the queenside and play the Blackmar-Diemer Gambit just for the hell of it, watching that big ol' forehead crease up into a thousand furrows. I go on to smash him in thirty-five moves.

As soon as I get out of the playing hall, Mom starts getting mad at me, yelling like a freak on a leash. She tells me she didn't fly us halfway around the world for me to play half-baked openings. Then it's Coach's turn, bawling me out for disrespecting Belgium's top grandmaster. He tells me I was deliberately staring at the guy's forehead to put him off. In my defense, I tell him, there was hardly any space in the playing hall NOT occupied by that forehead. Coach doesn't even crack a smile. Play the board, Leah, not the man, he mutters, which everyone knows is bull. It's not the board that wants to rip your head off and have it for dinner, is it? Anyways, look at the numbers. Four rounds, four wins, and my rating has gone up eighteen points already. You'd think they'd be happy. After all, I'm their creation.

COMMENTS

Roy: I like the occasional game of chess but I don't really understand this post. What's a Blackmar-Diemer Gambit? Please be clearer.

Chessgirl: What can I tell you, Roy? I'm an IM (International master) soon to be a GM (grandmaster) and it sounds like you're a patzer. I could play you blindfold with rook odds and thirty seconds on my clock and still take you apart. I'm not explaining the BDG to patzers. That's not what this blog is for. Clear enough for you?

Guppy: You don't sound like a very nice person, Chessgirl. And fyi, the Blackmar-Diemer Gambit has been proven unsound. GM Cornelius Hammett says that anyone who plays the

BDG in a tourno might as well climb onto the chessboard and ritually disembowel himself.

Chessgirl: Did Hammett say that before or after I beat him with Blackmar-Diemer at the Gibraltar Tradewise tournament back in 2011 when I was like ELEVEN YEARS OLD? Only one person got gutted that day and it wasn't me.

Socrates: You got a boyfriend?

Chessgirl: Drink hemlock, Socrates. Or go into exile. Your call.

Roy: Why are you so up yourself? Do you think people are going to read your blog if you insult your fellow chess players and everyone who comments?

Chessgirl: Douche.

Comments on this post are now closed.

50 THINGS ABOUT ME

1. The name Leah derives from the Hebrew word for 'weary'.

2. I don't have a middle name. If I did, I would want a Don't Mess With Me middle name like Scout or Jade.

3. I live with my mother on the first floor of an apartment block in Manhattan, New York.

4. I am seventeen years old. Just.

5. My birthday is April Fool's Day. That's right, my very existence is an April Fool's joke.

6. My dad is an engineer on the International Space Station. It takes him an hour and a half to orbit the Earth. He sees sixteen sunrises and sixteen sunsets every day.

7. I'm nothing like my dad. I'm scared of flying, which is bad because I have to travel by plane ALL THE TIME.

8. I'm scared of heights as well.

9. I found that out when I stayed at the JW Marriott Marquis hotel in Dubai. My room was on the sixty-ninth floor. I ended up sleeping behind a couch down in the hotel lobby.

10. I beat my first grandmaster when I was six years old. After the game he claimed he had toothache and wasn't thinking straight.

11. Beating a GM at chess is an amazing feeling. When he knocks his king over you feel a thrill that travels down your whole body and out through your toes.

12. I gave my first simultaneous chess exhibition when I was ten. I played forty strong club players. Won thirty, drew nine, lost one.

13. I got really mad about the one I lost. I thumped a pillar so hard I broke my hand.

14. Intelligence and irritability are a bad combination.

15. I once yelled 'Why am I losing to this idiot?!' during a tournament game in Milan. I got an official reprimand from the referee but I went on to win the game. And the tournament.

16. My cell phone ringtone is an mp3 of Bobby Fischer saying 'I love the moment when I crush a man's ego'.

17. I hate being asked whether there will ever be a female world chess champion. Of course there will.

18. Mom and Coach are convinced it's going to be me.

19. Today my chess rating is 2480. When I get to 2500 I will be a grandmaster.

20. When I'm studying chess positions at home I wear my crocodile onesie. I've had it for years. I cut the feet off so I wouldn't outgrow it.

21. One of my videos on YouTube has over a million hits: two GMs accidentally clashing heads over a chessboard, then cussing in Russian.

22. My best friend is called Rybka. We play chess together every day.

23. Rybka is a computer chess program.

24. My last boyfriend was Sergey, a Russian IM with floppy bangs. We started dating at the World Junior Championship three years ago.

25. He was my first boyfriend as well as my last.

26. I learnt dozens of obscure Russian proverbs to impress him with.

27. Shouldn't have bothered.

28. Now I have a rule about not dating chess players.

29. I'd break that rule for the right person.

30. I took my AP exams when I was sixteen. Aced them, obviously.

31. I was home-schooled, if you hadn't already guessed.

32. My home-school routine involved an average of five hours chess a day.

33. I once spent a whole night in my bedroom staring at a rook and pawn endgame. I didn't touch the pieces, but my mind was racing for seven hours straight.

34. I fear I have some sort of mental illness.

35. I feel sorry for anyone who thinks chess is boring. Chess gets its hooks into you and sends you crazy and ruins your life, but the one thing chess is not is boring.

36. My hero is the Latvian grandmaster Mikhail Tal. Replaying his best games is like swimming in chocolate.

37. Can't say I've ever swum in chocolate.

38. I swim in water every day. I can swim 50 meters in 40 seconds.

39. I can run a mile in five minutes flat.

40. I can jab a punchbag 74 times in 30 seconds.

41. I can jump rope 100 times before I screw up.

42. The reason I work out so much is that I need stamina for long chess games.

43. When I was fourteen my hair was so long I could sit on it.

44. Instead of sitting on it I cut it all off and sold it to a wigmaker for $80.

45. I invested the $80 in high-risk equity shares and now it's worth $254. Not even Mom knows about my Hair Money.

46. I like classical music: Bach, Beethoven and most of all Mahler.

47. I like the *Star Wars* music too. In fact, I like everything about *Star Wars*.

48. According to Chinese astrology, I'm a Metal Dragon, which means I can earn a lot of money in a very short time.

49. Chinese astrology is obviously a load of horsefeathers.

50. My sneezes sound like coughs. No one ever blesses me.

COMMENTS 💬

Kaixxo: Some fact checking needed here, methinks. The only Leah in the FIDE chess rankings is Leah Baxter, but there's no Baxter on the International Space Station. Either you're not really an IM or your father is not really in space.

Chessgirl: Or we don't share a surname. Or any one of a MILLION other possibilities.

Kaixxo: So what's his name then?

Chessgirl: His name is Yuri Blocked.

Guppy: Are you going to block everyone who calls you out for lying?

Comments on this post are now closed.

KNIGHT FALL

Round 5 in Pune and I've got black against a Serbian GM with a glass eye. The game is a Sicilian Dragon, Soltis variation. On move 31 I sacrifice a knight for positional advantage but Glass Eye finds all the right moves and my kingside attack runs out of steam. There's no way I can claw the material back and he goes on to grind out a win.

I leave the playing hall and walk to the elevator flanked by Mom and Coach, feeling like Princess Leia being escorted to the Emperor by imperial stormtroopers. They look so grim, it's almost funny.

'Why did you sacrifice that knight?' growls Coach. 'All the kibitzers in the green room said it was unsound.'

'It felt like the right thing to do.'

'Sacs don't always work out, Leah. Did you just feel it or did you calculate?'

'I calculated.'

'Did you spot the queen h4 line?'

'Sure.'

'So why d'you sac the knight?'

'It's what Mikhail Tal would have done.'

'He was Tal,' spits Coach, stabbing the elevator call button.

'Tal was Tal. Do you want me to make a note of that in my History of Chess notebook?'

Mom whirls around and chews me out. 'Don't you dare be sarcastic, Leah. Do you realize that we'd have GM ranking right now, if you hadn't decided to throw that game away?'

It's true. If I'd won today, I would have gained twenty-five rating points and I'd be a grandmaster right now.

The number above the elevator is stuck on 4. I stand there

staring at it, massaging the skin between my thumb and index finger.

'I think this elevator's broken,' I say.

But Mom's not done with me yet. 'Do you know how much it costs to fly three people from New York to Pune? Well, Leah, do you?'

'I'm going to take the stairs.'

'Don't walk away when I'm talking to you!' Mom yells after me. 'Do you have any idea how much I've sacrificed for you?'

'Guess Coach was right!' I shout back. 'Sacrifices don't always work out!'

I barge through the double doors and run down the steps three at a time. The stairwell reeks of disinfectant and samosas. I run straight to the basement gym and bench press one fifty pounds. Bam. Personal best.

COMMENTS

Roy: What is a kibitzer?

Chessgirl: Google it.

SirLancelot: Hey, Roy. You know how when you play a board game there's always someone looking over your shoulder offering unwanted advice and commentary? That's a kibitzer.

Comments on this post are now closed.

After lunch, Mom and Coach tell me I need therapy. Can you believe that? Five minutes on some dumbass psychology website and they figure they know my problem.

Self-sabotage. That's their diagnosis. They say that deep down I am afraid of winning. They say that every time I am on the edge of becoming a grandmaster I get scared and do something reckless. They say I'm not being beaten on the board, I'm being beaten by my Inner Critic.

Total horsefeathers, as Mom would say. Why would I need an inner critic when I've got perfectly destructive outer ones?

'You can still save your tournament,' drones Coach. 'You're playing White against Sivenko this afternoon. Play the quietest game you can. Strong and steady. Open with e4. Don't be a bull, be a boa constrictor. Crush her slowly.'

As Coach talks on and on, saying the same thing in a zillion different ways, I miss my dad more than ever. He always knows how to keep me calm on match days. He'll put a hand on my shoulder and do his mock-serious expression and give me meaningless advice to make me laugh. *If I were you, champ, I'd try the Kasparov Gambit today.* 'Dad, there's no such thing.' *So much the better! You'll have surprise on your side.*

My dad loves having a daughter who plays chess, and I love having a dad who doesn't.

Too bad he's in space.

Mom and Coach go to the green room and I go to the playing hall. Larissa Sivenko, the strongest GM in Ukraine, is sitting there already. She is eating a jelly donut and licking her fingers.

'Gross,' I say. 'You gonna shake with that hand?'

She frowns and holds out her fist to bump instead.

'Start your clocks,' announces the tournament director.

I have White, which is a big advantage at this level. I open with e4, strong and steady, just like Coach told me to. Sivenko thinks for a moment and brings out her kingside knight.

Alekhine's Defence. Typical.

Alekhine's Defence is named after Alexander Alekhine who was a total douche even for a chess player. He had a cat called Chess which he took with him to all his tournaments. They used to sit side by side and gaze at the board together deep in thought. And that's not all. Alekhine used to pee on the floor whilst sitting at the chessboard. I have literally no idea why he did that. But hey, he was one of the strongest players that ever walked the Earth. He spent *seventeen years* as World Champion. When you're that good, you can pee on the floor all morning if you want to and still sign autographs all afternoon.

People play Alekhine's Defence against me because they think I can't resist attacking early.

They're right. I can't.

I fling my pawns at Sivenko's knight, chasing it around the board from f6 to d5 to b6. And before my opponent has even finished her donut, I push my king's pawn another square forward, right down the throat of her position. It's the most aggressive book line I know against Alekhine's Defence, and I've played it in blitz chess more times than I can remember. The idea is to make your opponent gobble the pawn, then make her get slow, painful indigestion.

Sivenko is rattled. She hunches forward in her chair and sets about herself with a paper napkin, wiping sugar off her lips and sweat off her brow. The last morsel of donut sits untouched on her plate. I'm not exactly winning yet, but the game is razor sharp and she needs to find all the right moves if she's going to come out alive.

Tick-tock, tick-tock. That's right, Sivenko. Have a good think. If you take with the bishop, I'll fork you d5 and win a piece. If you take with the f pawn, I've got an open diagonal to your king.

I know that Mom and Coach are following my game on one of the big screens in the green room. This is the kind of position I love, but it's hardly what Coach had in mind when he said strong and steady. If I lose the game my life won't be worth living.

Sivenko thinks for twenty minutes, then captures with the f pawn. I lash out on the flank, pawn h4, smacking the clock button so hard it makes my opponent jump. She furrows her brow and thinks for another twenty minutes.

She has clearly never seen this position before, but I have. It's Mikhail Tal versus Bent Larsen, 1969. I studied it in my room a couple years ago, wearing my crocodile onesie same as always. In that game, Tal got a passed pawn on the a file. He should have won, but he didn't push the pawn fast enough and the game slipped away from him. I won't make the same mistake.

Tick-tock, tick-tock. Confidence surges through my arteries. I have used up eleven seconds on my clock and Sivenko has used up fifty *minutes*!

At last my opponent moves again, but instead of launching a counterattack like Larsen did against Tal, she plays pawn to g6, a weasely consolidating move. No, not weasely. Hedgehoggy. She's going to curl up into a tight prickly ball and pray I don't run her over.

I look up from the board, daring her to meet my gaze. *What's wrong, Sivenko? You scared?*

She refuses to look at me. She just stares at the board all hollow-eyed, dabbing her forehead with the napkin. But here's the thing. If you feel truly nervous during a game of chess, you do everything you can to try and hide it. You don't mop your brow like you're coming down with malaria.

You don't hyperventilate like a blonde in a slasher movie. You hide your distress.

I get it. The sly Ukrainian has been studying my Round 5 game, and she has reached the same diagnosis as Mom and Coach, that I'm into self-sabotage. She thinks her time-wasting and brow-mopping have fooled me. She's waiting for me to lunge forward, impale myself on her stupid spines and bleed out in agony all over the board.

I reach out and grab my kingside knight. *Come on then, Sivenko, let's see who bleeds out first.* I lift the knight high in the air, then freeze.

Fly high, Molotov Me!
Sky high, Molotov Me!

I close my eyes and try to force the Marsh Gibbons lyric from my mind. I have no idea where it came from – I don't even like the Marsh Gibbons – but the more I try to force it out, the louder it gets, until my head is full of noise like a juggernaut crunching gears.

This pleasure dome is doomed to fall
Molotov Me will sabotage it all!

Maybe they're right about me, Mom and Coach and Larissa Sivenko. Maybe I'm just a feckless kid, a Mikhail Tal wannabe with a flair for cheap tactical combos. Maybe I don't have what it takes to be a grandmaster.

Cry me a river in Memphis Mall
Molotov Me will sabotage it all!

Now that I've touched the knight, I have to move it somewhere, so I slam it down on g5. *Do your worst, donut girl.*

And she does.

And the game goes straight down the pan.

Over the course of the next two hours, Sivenko blunts the position, neutralizes every threat, forces a trade of queens and oozes through into the endgame with that extra pawn still in her sticky-fingered grasp. It's a passed pawn and her king is right in front of it, ready to escort it all the way to queendom. I'm in zugzwang. Any move I make right now is bad.

Blowing the farm on the Powerball
Molotov Me will sabotage it all!

There's nothing I hate more than losing with White. Having the first move is a big advantage at GM level, and White is expected to win or at least draw. When you lose with White, it feels like death.

It's not worth playing on, so I topple my king and we bump fists. Sivenko throws back her head and drops the last morsel of donut into her open mouth.

It's. Not. Worth. Playing. On. And if you think I'm just talking about the Sivenko game, you can think again. I'm done with chess.

COMMENTS

IbuprofenHarry: What is zugzwang?

Guppy: She already said what it is. It's when you reach a position on the board where every move available to you is a bad move. And Chessgirl, you're wrong about Alekhine peeing during matches. He peed on the carpet ONCE during a match in Malta (he was drunk at the time). And yes, he took his cat with him to most tournaments but not to all of them. Get your facts straight.

Chessgirl: Yeah, urination frequency and feline tournament attendance are totally what I care about right now. Why don't you come over to Pune and we'll hang out? We could talk about Russian cats and then slit our wrists together.

Juna: Sorry you've had a tough day, Chessgirl. I used to think I was really good at trampolining and then one day I watched some other girls trampolining and I realized I wasn't so good after all.

Chessgirl: Sorry, Juna, are you trying to draw some sort of parallel between your experience and mine? You and I clearly have access to some sort of keyboard. That's where our similarities end.

angus: don't give up, lassie. have you heard about that time when robert the bruce king of scotland lost a battle and went off to hide in a cave and saw a little spider making a web?

the little spider stopped what it was doing and looked straight at robert the bruce and said if at first you don't succeed try try again.

Chessgirl: No, laddie, I hadn't heard that version. Have you heard about capital letters?

Honeyboo: What Angus is trying to say is this. You've taken a knock, but you gotta get up again. You gotta get right back in the saddle. Stiffen the sinews! Summon up the blood! Go forth and show those booger-eating grandmasters what you're made of!

Chessgirl: Go forth yourself, Honeyboo, and please don't multiply.

Gibbonsfan1: Molotov Me kicks like a Klingon it's my favorite Marsh Gibbons track EVER gets me totally amped n banging my head like a billy goat and the best bit is right at the end when Axel D screams SABOTAGE IT AAAAAAAAAA AAAAAAAAAAAAALLLLLLLLLLLLLLLLL!!

Anonymous: Your dad's not in space, is he, Leah? Quit taking us for fools. If he died, just say he died. You're not the first person to experience grief.

Comments on this post are now closed.

THINGS I HATE AND THINGS TO DO

I'm on the way back to New York on the airplane. Here's a list of seven things I hate.

1. Flying
2. Sitting in the middle seat
3. India
4. Ukrainian grandmasters
5. Alekhine's Defence
6. Fighting back tears in public
7. Chess

And here's a list of seven things I can do now that I've given up chess.

1. Get a job (one that doesn't require deep thought)
2. Get a pet (I never had one before because I always had to travel so much)
3. Get a tattoo (I need to do something drastic to mark the start of my new life)
4. Get some friends
5. Get some sleep
6. Burn my chess books
7. Be normal

Mom and Coach don't know yet that I quit chess. I'm waiting for a good moment to tell them.

Hamsterlover: Get a hamster! They are so adorable and very smart for their size.

Chessgirl: Good idea. I might get several.

Hamsterlover: Coooooool!!! You won't regret it.

Chessgirl: How many hamsters does a royal python need each month?

Hamsterlover: I have reported your comment to the American Humane Association. You are a horrible person.

Socrates: Where u gonna get your tattoo?

Chessgirl: Manhattan.

Socrates: No, I meant where on your body?

Chessgirl: I know what you meant.

Tia: You shouldn't hate Ukrainian grandmasters. Just cos donut girl psyched you out doesn't mean they're all bad.

Comments on this post are now closed.

Mom: Please, Leah, don't do that. Don't quit now.

Coach: I tried to give up chess once. Lasted about three and a half hours.

COMMENTS 💬

Guppy: Your coach is right. You've been playing chess since you were five. Giving up is gonna be harder than you think.

SirLancelot: Can I have your chess books or did you burn them already?

Comments on this post are now closed.

HAIR MONEY

Back home in New York I cash in my Hair Money and use it to buy:

1. A cage with a sliding glass door
2. A thermostat and heating bulb
3. A royal python

Mom yells at me when I arrive home with the python. She says it will break out of its cage and kill us both in our sleep.

I keep my voice nice and quiet and give her all the reasons why snakes make perfect pets.

1. They don't smell
2. They don't drool
3. They don't hump your legs
4. They don't poop on the carpet
5. They don't claw the couch
6. They don't leave hairs all over your clothes
7. They don't eat you out of house and home

Mom picks up her tablet and starts searching. She wants stories of royal pythons bursting through toughened glass and swallowing teenage chess prodigies whole, but I'm pretty sure she won't find any. All she'll find out is how docile royal pythons are and how good their scales feel against your skin.

Ten minutes later she slams down the tablet and stalks out. 'Keep the snake if you want it so much!' she calls from the stairs. 'I hope it makes you very happy.'

I don't blame Mom for being mad at me. She wanted a grandmaster in her house and instead she wound up with a loser and a snake.

I put on my sneakers and baseball cap and go for a long run in Central Park. Not the boring asphalt loop that everybody runs, but the crazy winding trails off the Ramble, where there are rocks to jump on, streams to cross and mud to fall over in. It's awesome. You can totally forget you're in the city.

I come out onto 5th Avenue still feeling good so I run fifteen blocks down to Bryant Park, then another fifteen down to Madison Square Park. My body wants to stop but I carry on another fifteen blocks just to feel the pain. I run all the way to the fountain in Washington Square Park and stick my head under one of the water jets. My legs are Jell-o. My lungs are shot. I sit on the stone rim of the fountain and stare at the dumbass pigeons as they strut and peck. For a few beautiful minutes my mind is empty.

There's a chess shop on Thompson Street which I want to avoid, so I take the east gate out the park and run along Waverly Place and Greene Street. But then I run past a donut shop on the corner with 8th Street. It's called Gonuts Donuts and of course it reminds me of Larissa Sivenko and my epic fail in Pune.

I jog over to the shop, take off my cap and slump down right there on the sidewalk. *I shouldn't have forced the pace with knight g5. I should have gone for the slower move d5. I played like a patzer and got what I deserved.*

25

When I look up again there is a five-dollar bill in my cap.

'Hey, I'm not a bum!' I shout, but the people on the sidewalk are rushing to and fro like rats in a granary and no one pays me any attention.

You all know as well as I do that when the universe hands you five dollars outside a donut shop, it's bad luck not to spend it on donuts. So I get up and go into the shop.

The girl on the cash register grins at me like a loony from under her Gonuts Donuts cap. Behind her, a teenage boy is scrubbing down a worktop, breathing heavily. The back of his T-shirt reads 'All of New York is going nuts for our donuts', which clearly isn't true because the joint is half empty.

'Hi, Ronda,' I say, and the girl looks totally amazed, like I recited her family tree right back to the Founding Fathers. 'Your name's on the badge,' I add.

The girl facepalms. 'Sorry, keep forgetting. What can I get you?'

'Iced coffee and two cinnamon donuts.'

That's what I should have done. Push the d pawn and let her exchange knights. If she castles, I play bishop d3 and follow up with pawn h5 as soon as possible.

STAFF NEEDED. The notice on the counter catches my eye and my brain jolts like it does when I spot a mate in four moves. 'I want to apply for that job,' I hear myself say.

'Awesome!' Ronda grins from ear to ear. 'We could sure use some help around here, couldn't we, Michael?'

The boy stares at me glumly through thick glasses. 'I guess.'

I smile. 'That's settled then. When do I start?'

Ronda bursts out laughing and flaps her hand in a You're-Too-Much kind of way. She hurries off to a back room and returns with the manager, a thin black man with worry lines on his forehead. He looks me up and down and the worry lines turn into scowl lines. 'You've got nerve,' he whispers.

'Sir?'

'Piece of advice, missy. When you apply for a job as a crew member at a baked goods establishment, you do NOT show up covered in sweat and mud.'

'Think of it as glaze and sprinkles, sir.'

The manager tries to look serious but his scowl lines are twitching and wriggling all over the place and I know the job is mine if I want it.

COMMENTS

Leo: Why would a genius apply for a job in a donut shop?

Chessgirl: Penance. Earn absolution by serving donuts to idiots.

Anonymous: Did you know there are chess tables on the southwest corner of Washington Square Park? You must have been really close. You could have gone there for a game or two!

Chessgirl: There are only four kinds of people who play chess in parks: patzers, gamblers, junkies and has-beens.

Dreadnought5: You'd fit right in, then. Sounds to me like you're a has-been.

BarbaraB: I am totally addicted to donuts but my local donut store is closed for renovation.

Chessgirl: Probably putting in wider doors for you.

Roy: Service industries are about being nice to people and making them feel good. Congratulations on the job and all. You won't last five seconds.

Comments on this post are now closed.

AFTERNOON BAKE

I've been working at Gonuts Donuts for three days now. I start at 2 p.m. and finish at 10 p.m. and my duties are as follows:

1.   Serve on the front counter with Ronda and Michael
2.   Assist with the afternoon bake

3.   Fill donut shells with jelly
4.   Add glaze and sprinkles
5.   Wipe surfaces, sweep floors, wash dishes
6.   Bag up day-old donuts for the homeless

The manager and chief baker of Gonuts Donuts is called Randal Johnson. And I just found out that Ronda is his daughter, though she calls him 'sir', just like everyone else.

Randal keeps reminding me of the Gonuts First Commandment: 'Smile at customers till your cheeks ache'. And the Gonuts one-two-three, which are as follows:

No more than ONE minute between taking a customer's payment and handing them their order.

No more than TWO donuts at a time on the jelly dispenser.

No more than THREE donuts per day to be consumed by any crew member, and only in the back room, never at the counter.

Randal yells at me from time to time, but only in the back room and not half as much as Mom and Coach used to. And Ronda keeps saying how quickly I'm learning the ropes. Of course, if she knew I'd got four and a half thousand annotated GM chess games stacked up in my memory, she might not be so impressed at my remembering where the toasted coconut lives.

I haven't told any of my colleagues about my former life. They think I'm normal.

Anonymous: Meet it is that I set down: one may smile and smile and be a villain.

Chessgirl: Wot?

Anonymous: Bake, glaze, smile all you like, it doesn't change who you are. Three more days without the adrenalin rush of competition and you'll shrivel up and die.

Chessgirl: Who are you?

Anonymous: A well-wisher.

Chessgirl: Wish off.

Comments on this post are now closed.

BARREL

I'm writing this post on my phone because my tablet is broken. All I want to say is this: My mother is crazy. Screwy. Wacko.

At breakfast time she corners me in the kitchen and starts hollering about wasted talent. 'Why have you given up?' she yells. 'Did Magnus Carlsen give up when Giri beat him with Black in twenty-two moves? Did Nakamura give up when he crashed out of the London Chess Classic without winning a single game? Did Judit Polgár give up when Kasparov lectured her on the "imperfections of the feminine psyche"? Of course not. They persevered, all of them, and attained true greatness.'

What she doesn't mention, of course, is that Polgár was fifteen when she attained her GM title. Nakamura was fourteen. Carlsen was thirteen.

Mom seems to think that seventeen is young.

SEVENTEEN. IS. ANCIENT.

'You're still upset about Pune,' Mom goes on. 'But your opponents didn't beat you on the board. They beat you in your head.'

In my head! That's rich. She has no idea how complex those games in Pune were. The Sivenko game was a warren a hundred million miles deep and Mom should be grateful she wasn't the poor sucker that got sent down there.

'Your head can be fixed, Leah.' Mom forces a smile. 'With a bit of therapy and neural programming, your head can be fixed.'

She waddles toward me as if to hug me, but I duck under her outstretched arms. 'Fix your own head!' I yell. 'Fix your own head and then we'll talk about mine!'

It's time, I think. If I don't do it now, I never will. So I run to my room, grab all my chess books off the shelves and sprint back through the hallway, balancing the books in a teetering pile between hands and chin.

'Leah, what are you doing? Come back here!'

Mom's squawky voice follows me down the corridor, through the back door and into the yard.

I drop the books into the barrel that we use for burning leaves and yard waste. Then I go to the shed and fetch a box of matches and a four-gallon canister of gasoline.

'Leah!' Mom's voice is the voice of a deranged woman. Here she comes, flying out into the yard, peroxide hair crazy in her wake.

I unscrew the top of the canister and begin to pour.

'Leah, stop!' She flies toward me and then (how's this for crazy?) she leaps into the barrel.

I stop pouring. The acrid smell of gasoline is thick in the air. There she stands, right there in the barrel with the yard waste and the chess books, her face contorted with grief and rage.

'Get out of the barrel, Mom.'

'No.' She glares at me through a mist of tears.

'They're my books.'

'You're not yourself, Leah. You love these books.'

'I hate them.'

Her hands are on mine now, trying to prize my fingers off the canister handle. '*My 60 Memorable Games* by Bobby Fischer, signed first edition,' she whispers. 'Your father gave you that when you won the Milan Open.'

'Don't bring Dad into this.'

'He gave you this one too, didn't he?' She points with a foot. '*A Guide to Poisoned Pawn Openings.* You used to carry it everywhere with you.' With a violent tug she wrests the canister from my grasp. A slug of gasoline spews from the canister and splashes over her blouse, skirt and stockings.

I look down at the box of matches in my hand.

'Leah?' croaks Mom, and the crazy in her voice is tinged with sudden fear. 'Leah, give me the matches.'

What have we come to? What sort of a lunatic does she think I am?

I turn and run into the apartment, run to my room, lock the door, fling myself on my bed, grab my tablet computer and log onto chess.com. Within two seconds some patzer in Germany is challenging me to a game.

I lift the tablet high into the air and smash it down hard onto the corner of my bedside table. The screen splinters into a web of tiny shards and then goes dark.

COMMENTS

Ringo: It's not just your mom who's insane. You're as crazy as a box of frogs.

Fungusface: Ahahaha, I thought my family was dysfunctional. GET OUT OF THE BARREL MOM! Priceless.

SirLancelot: How much gasoline went on the books? If they're still in readable condition, I'll give you twenty bucks for the lot.

Guppy: Carlsen was thirteen when he *qualified* for a GM norm, but he wasn't officially awarded GM status until the FIDE conference later that year, by which time he was fourteen. Get your facts straight.

Chessgirl: Thank you all for your support at this difficult time.

Comments on this post are now closed.

PHOENIX

In Greek mythology the phoenix was a crested bird. Its eyes were blue as sapphires and the scales on its legs were shining gold. Every thousand years or so, the phoenix died in a dramatic explosion of flames and then rose again from the ashes of its former self.

Walking away from chess is the biggest thing I've ever done.

The old me has crashed and burned, and now the new me will rise. I have a picture in my mind of a white king lying on its side on a chessboard. Rising out of the cold dead body of that king is a beautiful phoenix with red and yellow tail feathers.

Resurrection. That's what I'm going to have on my tattoo.

COMMENTS

Sandra: Sounds gorgeous, Chessgirl. Don't forget to post pictures!

Gorgon: Getting my tattoo was the best thing I ever did. You won't regret it.

Don: Tattooing a minor is illegal in New York, even with parental permission. No reputable artist is gonna let you go under the needle.

Gorgon: Wear heels and a bit of makeup. They won't even ask the question lol.

Hakunamatata: How's the snake? Has it got a name yet?

Chessgirl: Anatoly. And before anyone asks, no, he's not named after Anatoly Karpov. I just figure Anatoly is a good name for a snake, okay?

Comments on this post are now closed.

A weirdo walks into Gonuts Donuts in the middle of my shift.

'Land!' he cries, and plonks himself down on a stool at the counter.

'Hello,' I say. 'How may I help you?'

The weirdo looks about my age. He pushes back his long hair and stares at me. At least, I think he's staring at me. There's something wonky about his eyes, like they can't agree which direction to look.

'*They came unto a land,*' he whispers, '*in which it seemed always afternoon.*'

'Riiiight.'

'And around about the counter with faces pale, the mild-eyed melancholy donut-eaters came.'

'Uh-huh,' I say. 'Did you just escape from somewhere? Is there someone I should be calling?'

'No thanks, Leah.' He leans forward on the counter and beams at me.

'You want a donut?' I say. 'Coffee?'

'Your name means weary, doesn't it?'

'Er – yes.'

36

'And are you weary?' He jerks his head to indicate the shop and its contents. 'Of this.'

'Not at all,' I lie. 'I love it.'

'What do you love about it?'

'Everything. The smell of the bake, the ring of the cash register, the smiles, the small talk, the little noises that people make when they take their first bite of a freshly baked donut.'

'What sort of noises?'

'Sighs of pleasure. They can't help themselves.'

'Like this?' He closes his eyes and starts moaning in ecstasy. Everyone in the shop turns and stares at us.

'Stop it,' I hiss. 'You're disturbing the customers.'

'I'm rousing them from their mild-eyed melancholy.'

'You're putting them off their food.'

He leans forward and puts his hand on my wrist. 'What about the money?' he whispers. 'Is the money good?'

I snatch my hand away. 'None of your business.'

'Come and work for me.'

'What?'

'Quit your job. I'll make it worth your while.'

'No!'

I don't hear Randal arrive from the back room but suddenly he is right beside me, his voice quiet and menacing. He's telling the weirdo in no uncertain terms that his attentions are not welcome. The word 'harassment' is used.

'All right. I'm going.' The weirdo puts his hands high above his head and marches to the door. 'Checkmate,' he says, and leaves.

COMMENTS

Delphi: What a jerk. He won't bother you anymore.

Lisa: 'The Lotos-Eaters' is my favorite poem EVER. If a boy recited 'The Lotos-Eaters' to me and then told me to quit my job, I'd say yes.

Sandra: I totally do that sigh thing when I bite into a fresh-baked donut.

Skipperbekker: Me too, hehe. Mine's more of a grunt than a sigh.

Forgetmenot: Checkmate? Sounds to me like he knows exactly who you are.

Comments on this post are now closed.

Tuesday.

Before I even get out of bed I watch a bunch of YouTube tutorials about how to make yourself look older. As soon as Mom leaves on her daily job-hunting expedition, I raid her makeup box and get busy. I put dark blush under my cheekbones and down the sides of my nose. I apply gray eye shadow and a ton of black eyebrow pencil. I borrow clothes from her wardrobe, taking care to choose clothes she won't miss: a pencil skirt, an old jacket and black high-heeled boots.

In ten minutes, I age ten years.

I take the subway to the tattoo parlor, press my phone to my ear and walk into the shop, cool as you like. 'I don't care which courier you use,' I bark into the phone. 'Just make sure the file is with me by three thirty. No excuses.'

The receptionist looks at me coldly. 'Can I help you?'

'Sure.' I glance at my watch. 'Is Mick free for a prelim right now?'

Prelim. I've been reading tattoo blogs. I know all the jargon.

She glances down at her book. 'Can you wait ten minutes?'

Easy as that. The receptionist writes down my name and address and a few other details, but she doesn't ask my age.

Ten minutes later, I am sitting in the tattoo parlor. There are tattoo pics all over the walls, a high couch in the middle of the room, and two chairs either side of a messy desk.

'I want a chess piece on my back,' I say, taking a white king out of Mom's purse and laying it on the desk between us.

'No problem,' Mick says. 'Upper or lower back?'

'Lower.'

'You sure you want him lying down like that?'

'Yes.'

'Like the game's been lost?'

'You got a problem with that?'

'Not at all.'

'Yes, you do,' I say. 'You think it's un-American.'

'This isn't about what I think.' Mick pulls a piece of paper toward him. 'It's about what's right for you.' He bends his head and sketches the outline of a king. He draws quickly and well, and I sit there feeling bad for being obnoxious. 'What about a black king instead?' he says suddenly. 'Black chess pieces look good on pale skin. I can shade the contours and add tiny spots of light along the edges.'

'No. It's got to be white.'

'Light ink hurts more than dark ink.'

'I don't care.'

'You will.'

The lights flicker and the walls close in on me, echoing with the screams of yesterday's customers. Okay, not that exactly. Just an awkward silence during which Mick realizes he needs to work on his bedside manner.

'It's a straightforward design,' he says. 'We'll fix a day and you'll be in and out within two hours.'

'There's more,' I say. 'I need a multi-colored phoenix rising out of the dead king.'

Mick turns his pen box upside down, scattering felt-tip pens all over the desk. 'Now you're talking!' he beams. 'Make that five hours.'

He draws a bunch of phoenix samples and I choose the one I like best. I make an appointment with the receptionist and walk out of the shop feeling like a gazillion bucks.

Can't WAIT to have it on my skin.

COMMENTS

Don: You're conning a professional artist into breaking the law. I hope your tattoo gets infected.

Chessgirl: Shucks, Don, you say the sweetest things.

Bodyart2: Light ink and dark ink both hurt exactly the same, but the light ink gets added toward the end of the session, by which time the skin is already tender. So light ink doesn't hurt more, it just feels like it does.

Chessgirl: 'Light ink doesn't hurt more, it just feels like it does.' Do you people actually *read* your comments before posting?

Gorgon: Well done, you! I told you the makeup and heels would do the trick. When are you booked in for inking?

Chessgirl: Friday at ten. Wish me luck!

Anonymous: Don't do it. Chess is part of who you are. You will play chess again for sure one day and you'll wish you'd never got that dumb tattoo.

Comments on this post are now closed.

BORED

You won't believe who came into Gonuts Donuts in the middle of my shift today. No, not the Lotos-Eater.

Mom.

She waddles into the shop with her hair in a bun and asks Ronda for a large coffee and a Coconut Cahuna. I'm busy with another customer, but I can't help glancing over at

Mom. She gives me a double thumbs-up sign and grins fatuously like a kids' TV show host. Then she goes to a table by the window and settles into a chair with her donut and her coffee. She flashes me another grin, takes a book out of her bag and pretends to read. I turn my back to her and start filling donuts.

This is messing with my head. Not long ago Mom was sitting in a flashy hotel in Milan, watching me compete in the final of a prestigious chess tournament, brooding over my performances like a jealous dragon over gold. And now what? She's watching me shove fried doughballs two by two onto the spikes of a raspberry jelly dispenser. She's not reading that book of hers, she's reading the inane slogan on the back of my T-shirt: *All of New York is going nuts for our donuts.*

I can't bear it any longer. I flick the jelly dispenser to idle, grab a jug of coffee and head over to Mom's table. She peers over the top of her book, watching me approach.

'What are you doing here, Mom?'

'I was passing.'

'No, you weren't. Do you want me to feel ashamed of working here? Is that your plan?'

'Not at all.' She dabs her mouth with a paper napkin. 'I just want you to be happy, Leah. Tell me, do you judge for

43

yourself when the donut shells are full of jelly, or does the machine do it for you?'

'The machine does it,' I say, my voice rising. 'All I do is set the machine to twelve, shove two donuts on the spikes, reach across with my pinkie and press FILL.'

'Sounds tricky.'

'It's not tricky.' My heart is thumping in my chest. 'There isn't an iota of trickiness in anything I do here. Not the teeniest morsel of skill. And guess what? I'm okay with that. So if you think you're going to shame me into quitting my job and taking up chess again, you're wrong.'

Someone is standing right behind me, clearing his throat. I turn around and see a mosaic of scowl lines. It's the boss.

'Remind me, Leah,' says Randal. 'What's the Gonuts First Commandment?'

'Smile at customers till your cheeks ache. But sir, this isn't a customer, this is my mom.'

'Is that so?' Randal takes the coffee jug from me. 'Pleased to meet you, Mrs Baxter. More coffee, on the house?'

'Just a drop, Mr—'

'Johnson.' He pours. 'More toasted coconut for your Cahuna?'

'No, thank you.'

Randal gives me back the coffee jug. 'Honor your father and mother, Leah, that you may live long in the land. And when you've properly apologized to your mother, go and see if the new donut shells are ready.'

Honor your father and mother. If only I had the chance.

Randal stays there, waiting.

'Sorry, Mom,' I say, pinching the skin between my thumb and index finger until it hurts.

COMMENTS

Luther88: Ahahahaha, you got owned!

RadyM: Your boss rocks.

Donutpro: You're a loser, Chessgirl. You flunked chess and now you're flunking donuts. As a donut retailer with twenty years' experience I can tell you there's a ton of skill involved in what we do. Making good coffee is a skill. Glazing a donut neatly is a skill. Putting people at ease is a skill.

Chessgirl: Tracing a blog comment to a street address is a skill.

Donutpro: I'm reporting you to the NYPD for making a substantive threat on my life.

Chessgirl: Ahahahahahaha.

Comments on this post are now closed.

Mom's not so bad. In fact, she has moments of being almost normal. Also, it looks like her job-hunting expeditions have finally paid off. She's got herself a receptionist job at a driving school in Lower East Side. Starts next Monday.

We celebrate by making pizza for dinner and then snuggling up on the couch to watch TV. I wear my crocodile onesie.

We start off watching re-runs of the *George Lopez Show*, but that makes Mom cry, so we switch channels and watch the second half of *The Joy Luck Club* instead.

Not a single argument all evening. And Mom called me munchkin twice, which she hasn't done in months.

COMMENTS 💬

Skipperbekker: Sorry Chessgirl but if we wanted charming domestic posts like this one we'd be reading the Family Focus blog.

Ringo: Congrats on your mom's new job and all, but Skipperbekker is right. We come here to watch you destroy yourself and to laugh at your dysfunctional chessmom. Have some respect for your audience.

Lisa: Ignore the trolls, Chessgirl. I'm glad you had a special evening with your mom.

Comments on this post are now closed.

BOBBY

Friday morning dawns and I arrive in Greenwich Village way too early. I still have a full hour before my tattoo appointment, plenty of time for a visit to West 10th Street.

I stroll along the tree-lined street and stop outside Number 23, a narrow townhouse. It looks just like all the other houses and if you didn't know its history you would walk right past it. Not me, though. I hop up onto the low wall across the street from The House and sit there with my chin in my hands, gazing at the ornate iron railings, the vast bay window, the three steps down to the entrance and that small bronze plaque engraved with tiny lettering: THE MARSHALL CHESS CLUB.

In 1956 this place would have looked much the same as it does now. It doesn't take much to imagine thirteen-year-old Bobby Fischer shuffling up this street behind his mother, corduroyed and bryl-creamed and ready to play. He lollops down the steps, along a corridor and into a smoke-filled tournament room. He plonks himself down on his chair across the board from the great Donald Byrne, scrawls the date at the top of his tournament playsheet, adjusts the black pieces minutely on their squares and reaches out for an awkward, gangly handshake.

Bobby is as nervous as a cat in a room full of rocking chairs. Sure, his IQ is higher than Einstein's and sure, he's memorized a thousand classic games, but the men in this room are some of the best chess players in the world. His opponent today is known to be an incredibly aggressive attacker. This is the biggest test of skill young Bobby has ever encountered.

Donald Byrne plays White. He grabs the center of the board with his pawns and the young Bobby Fischer counters on the flanks. Classic Grünfeld Defence until move 11 when Bobby plays a novelty, knight to a4, a bold and ungainly advance. His opponent steeples his fingers across his brow and thinks for fifteen minutes before responding. On move seventeen Bobby plays an even gutsier move, giving up his queen in exchange for a bishop. The seemingly insane sacrifice draws a gasp of astonishment from club secretary Edward Lasker standing behind him.

What happens next is pure Hollywood. The thirteen-year-old kid in the stripy shirt and corduroy pants unleashes an attack so deep and irresistible that it will be studied all around the world for decades to come. He coordinates his knights, bishops and rooks with terrifying precision and unleashes a windmill of discovered checks that devastates his opponent's position. Byrne plays on sportingly until the end but his queen has no chance against the bloodthirsty army that confronts her. On move forty-one Bobby seals the deal and scrawls *Mate* on the bottom of his playsheet.

Bobby Fischer's win that day is still known as 'the Game of the Century' and one grandmaster called move 11 – Na4 – 'the most powerful move in the history of chess'. In the following weeks and months Bobby went on to kick the ass of every grandmaster in the world.

So here's the thing, folks. Right after the Milan Open, a New York chess magazine ran a feature about me comparing my attacking style of play to that of the young Bobby Fischer. I framed the feature and hung it on the wall of my room (who wouldn't, right?) and ever since then I've been making pilgrimage to Number 23 West 10th Street. I can't count the number of times I've sat on this here wall, plotting to take over the world.

Except today.

This isn't pilgrimage. This is goodbye.

COMMENTS 💬

Dingbat: Bobby Fischer was a psycho and you know it. At the age of six he got expelled from school for kicking the principal. By the age of nine he'd been in and out of six different schools. At the age of fourteen (the year AFTER the Game of the Century) he bit a chess rival's arm so deep it never healed up. At seventeen he kicked his mother out of the family home and lived there on his own from that day on. Great role model, huh?

Chessgirl: I never said he was a great role model. I said he was a great chess player. Maybe the Greatest Of All Time.

Luther88: Every time a young American chess player does well in an international tournament, some swivel-eyed hack pops up and writes a thousand words of flag-waving horse manure under the headline COULD THIS BE THE NEXT BOBBY FISCHER? Shows how desperate we are for another home-grown chess champ. The fact that you took the article seriously just shows how arrogant and deluded you are, Chessgirl.

Guppy: Flag-waving horse manure? Mixed metaphor LMAO.

Sigurd: Wind your neck in, Luther88. Chessgirl is the real deal, a genuine prodigy. When she was ten she played a forty-board simul at the Manhattan Chess Club and lost just ONE GAME. The ten-year-old Bobby Fischer never did that.

Luther88: Who are you, her mom?

Ringo: Pointless argument, peeps. She already quit chess. Ten years from now she'll be propping up the bar in some crummy liquor joint, mumbling 'I used to be the next Bobby Fischer' to anyone who'll listen.

Comments on this post are now closed.

I arrive at the tattoo parlor all excited. It's not just about the tattoo, of course, it is about reinventing myself. Proving to myself and to the world that there is life after chess and that I'm not just a pawn for other people to push around.

When I go in, the receptionist looks up at me, even colder than before.

'I'm seeing Mick at ten,' I say.

'No, you're not,' she says. I try to show her my appointment card, but she doesn't even glance at it. 'We got a phone call warning us about you. Gave us your blog address and everything.'

'Oh.'

'You could have gotten us into a lot of trouble, Leah.' She walks to the door and opens it for me. 'Come back when you're eighteen.'

I go out onto the sidewalk and double over. *What just happened?*

'Sucks, doesn't it?' said a voice.

I turn and see the weirdo from the donut shop. He is wearing a lime green T-shirt and leaning against a lamppost.

'I know how you feel,' says the weirdo. 'I got thrown out of a shop once. The feelings of rejection were crushing.'

I straighten up. 'It was you, wasn't it? You've been reading my blog. You made that phone call.'

'Yeah.' He folds his arms. 'Good job on the makeup, though. You look at least twenty-two.'

'How did you know which tattoo parlor to call?'

'I rang around all of them, asking to speak to Mick. Got lucky on the fifth try.'

'Why d'you do it?'

'How about I tell you over a milkshake?' His wonky eyes twinkle and he grins at me like a shot fox.

So I slug him.

Yeah, that's right, I slug him on the jaw and he goes down BAM like a patzer's king, and the next thing I know he's lying on the sidewalk with a bloody lip, cussing and moaning and trying not to cry.

'Here's an idea,' I say. 'How about we skip the milkshake and you tell me now instead?'

COMMENTS 💬

Guppy: And . . . ?

Chessgirl: And that's all, folks. I'm sorry to leave you high and dry, but we can't go on like this. It freaks me out that somebody looked at this blog and started interfering with my life. There's no way I'm going to let that happen again. I'm going to password protect my next post and every single post after that, and I'm only giving the password to really awesome people who I totally trust.

Guppy: Like who?

Chessgirl: Nobody.

Tarantella: You can't just go about hitting people, however mad they've made you feel.

Chessgirl: Oops.

Tarantella: I'm serious. Violence is the weapon of the weak. You're better than that, Chessgirl.

Chessgirl: I'm really not.

Fagin2: I love reading your snarky blog posts. Can I have the password, please?

Chessgirl: No. Farewell, sweet world.

Comments on this post are now closed.

PART TWO: MIDDLEGAME

When I am White I win because I am White.
When I am Black I win because I am Bogoljubov.

Efim Bogoljubov (1889–1952)

It's a pity the public blog didn't work out. I enjoyed writing about my life and reading all the dumbass comments. But I've made my decision: every post from now on is going to be password-protected. I'd rather be a nobody than have people stalking me.

I do want to keep writing, though. At the end of a long lousy day there's nothing better than sitting down at a laptop and writing five thousand words of rambling self-justification. Hey, when I'm in the mood I can write ten posts in a single sitting without even getting up to pee. Superhuman stamina, that's what I've got. The ability to sit and concentrate for seven hours straight. If there were awards for concentration, I'd be right at the front of the line.

So where was I?

Oh yes, Guppy and Tarantella and a bunch of other rubbernecks want to know what's eating me up. They want to know why I wound up slugging a weirdo outside a tattoo parlor. I don't know the answer to that, but perhaps these six zingers have something to do with it:

1. My dad is not an astronaut and never was. He worked in the math department at NYU.

2. He died seven hundred and eighty-one days ago and it still feels like yesterday.

3. I'd never even heard of pancreatitis until he got it.

4. The doctors told us he wouldn't die. A simple routine operation went very wrong.

5. Mom got a big-ass compensation pay-out from the hospital.

6. She spent the money taking me to a bunch of international tournaments. I crashed and burned in every single one.

WHAT HAPPENED AFTER I PUNCHED THE WEIRDO

So the weirdo is spitting and groaning on the sidewalk, and I'm sitting next to him trying not to feel guilty and pretty much succeeding.

'What's your name?' I ask him.

'Kit McTarnsay,' he moans. 'I play chess in Washington Square Park.'

'What's that got to do with me?'

'I lead a gang called the Poisoned Pawns. We want you to join us.'

'You want me to be in your gang?' I laugh. 'Get outta here.'

'It's not a gang so much as a syndicate. We play chess for money and we share our winnings.'

'You're chess hustlers?'

'Exactly. We challenge all-comers to play blitz and bullet chess at five dollars a pop.'

'Win much?'

'Enough.' He lifts his shirt, unzips a money belt and rifles a sheaf of fifties. 'Last week's earnings.'

I'm not laughing anymore. I wouldn't earn that in a month at Gonuts Donuts.

'Last week,' says Kit, 'I was watching chess videos on YouTube and I came across one of yours. Two GMs clashing heads over the board and cussing in Russian. I followed the link to your blog and I became—'

'– a stalker.'

'Became interested in your life. I'll admit it, I felt sorry for you. All that pressure from your mom and your coach, when all you wanted to do was to play the game you love. I totally get you, Leah. I get why you quit competitive chess and I get why you got a job in a donut and coffee joint and I get why you're bored of it already. I just wanted to offer you a way out.'

'By reciting "The Lotos-Eaters" and sabotaging my tattoo appointment.'

'I couldn't let you go ahead with the tattoo. It's one thing to fall out of love with chess for a little while. It's another thing to go and ink it on your skin. *No ocean wide has drops enough to wash foul-tainted flesh.* Can't argue with Macbeth.'

I stop walking and look at him. 'What's your chess rating?'

'Twenty-one hundred.'

'You know chess hustling is illegal, right?'

'Keeping a royal python in New York City is illegal. Tattooing a minor is illegal. Punching people in the face is illegal. All I'm asking is that you come and see us play. Whatever you decide after that is fine.'

I bite my lip and my brain goes into chess mode, calculating possibilities at a hundred miles an hour. 'Some of the park players are ex-circuit. I'd be recognized.'

Kit laughs. 'With all that makeup, nobody's going to recognize you. And just to make sure' – he shrugs off his backpack and delves inside – 'you'll be wearing this.'

He holds out a long red wig. Douchebag came prepared.

PARK

As we approach the chess tables in Washington Square Park, Kit turns to me and says, 'Kiss me, quick.'

'What? Why?'

'Cover story,' says Kit. 'You're my girlfriend. We met at a music festival in Brooklyn and fell in love.'

'I've got a better cover story. You be you, and I'll be the girl that's about to ram a whole set of Staunton chess pieces where the sun don't shine.'

'Okay, no cover story. Just two people in the park. One of whom has a rule about not dating chess players.'

'Exactly.'

'Although you'd break that rule for the right person.'

'I'll break your legs if you quote my blog at me again.'

The chess tables are buzzing with joyous, chaotic games, not at all like the stuffy tournament matches I'm used to. I thrill to the clicking of the pieces on the board, the rattle of chess clocks being tapped and the murmuring and cussing of kibitzers.

'I'll point out the Poisoned Pawns,' whispers Kit, 'but don't say a word to any of them, okay? No one knows we're working together.'

There are about fifteen people standing around the tables. They jeer and harrumph and pass crumpled five-dollar bills in fingerless gloves.

'See that kid over there?' says Kit, pointing. A black kid in a T-shirt and baseball cap is playing standing up. He is bouncing up and down on the balls of his feet and jabbering away to his opponent.

'Nathan Banks,' whispers Kit. 'Youngest player in the park. Poisoned Pawn.'

'Rating?'

'Hard to say. In classical chess he'd be no more than two thousand. Put him in a tourney and he'll get taken apart like a patzer. But at blitz I've seen him beat guys rated twenty-two hundred. He's lightning fast, see. Faster than anyone I've seen. Wait till you see him play an opening or endgame – his fingers are a total blur. Keeps the pressure on his opponents, and all the while he's getting inside their heads with his trash talk. Listen.'

We drift over and join the crowd standing around the table.

'Too weak, too slow,' says Nathan, waggling his finger in his opponent's face. 'Castle while you can, fish, I'm coming for ya. Too weak, too slow. Clock's ticking, fish! What you got now? You serious? You didn't wanna do that. I'm coming for ya, fish. What you got? What you got? You're floundering, fish. What you got? Boom! Five bucks less, that's what you got.'

'If he ever talks to me like that,' I whisper to Kit, 'I'll knock his teeth down his throat.'

'I'll let him know,' Kit whispers.

We wander over to another table, where a blonde girl in sunglasses is playing an old man.

'Anna Ivanova,' Kit murmurs in my ear. 'Twenty-one years old. Poisoned Pawn. Came to the US from Russia. She's in her final year of university across the road from here and plays in the park every vacation to finance her studies. You'll love watching her, Leah, she's just like Karpov used to be. Nothing flashy about her, but no blunders either. We call her Anna Anaconda because she grabs you right out of the opening and squeezes the life out of you bit by bit. Takes all the air out of your position and then dives in for the kill. Pure class.'

'Rating?'

'Twenty-two hundred, maybe more. And there's nothing more off-putting than being trash talked in Russian.'

I look up from Anna's game and spot a tall, skinny kid at the furthest table. He's wearing a *Star Wars* T-shirt, gray Reeboks and a New York Giants baseball cap.

'Hey, that's Spencer Fawkes,' I say. 'Is he one of your lot?'

'For now,' says Kit. 'You two know each other?'

'Played him in the New York Open a couple of years ago. Queen's Gambit. Beat him in a rook pawn endgame. What's he rated these days?'

'Twenty-one eighty-five in classical chess, but you wouldn't think so to watch him play blitz. Between you and me, he hasn't got the stomach for it. He gets into time trouble and stutters when he trash talks. Breaks even some of the time, but costs us money most days.'

'You going to ditch him?'

'Depends.' Kit turns to face me. 'Will you take his place?'

And there it is. The big question. Do I want to be The Girl Who Used to Play Classical Chess in International Tournaments and Now Plays Blitz with Patzers in the Park?

'I don't know,' I say. 'Let me play a game or two and think about it.'

BLITZ

Speed has always been a New York thing. We walk fast, we talk fast, we work fast, we shop fast, we eat fast, we speed date. We got things to do, money to make, people to offend. It's no surprise that speed chess began right here in New York.

The first 'rapid transit' chess tournaments had a time limit of thirty seconds a move, which then went down to ten seconds a move. Poor old ref had to stand on a chair with a clock and a bell. He rang it every ten seconds and if you didn't move in time you lost the game.

A hundred years ago the speed tournaments were bossed by one man, the Cuban chess machine José Raúl Capablanca.

He didn't just win, he wiped his opponents off the board so fast it made their heads spin.

After fifty years of referees teetering on chairs, someone invented a chess clock with two timers and a button above each one. You make your move, you press the button, your opponent's timer starts ticking. *Click, clack, click, clack*, that was (and still is) the unmistakable sound of a speed chess tourney at the Manhattan Chess Club. These clocks don't have a 'per move' limit, just one time control for each player for the entire game. Fifteen minutes for rapid chess. Five minutes for blitz chess. One minute for bullet chess. If your flag drops you lose the game, regardless of the position on the board.

My hero Mikhail Tal was an absolute wizard at speed chess, so quick and so brilliant that Boris Spassky used to call him the F1 racer. Losing to Tal at blitz must have been like getting run over by a Ferrari. You're lying mangled on the road but in the midst of all the pain you're thinking, Gee, cool car.

Three more zingers for you, Diary dear:

1. Reincarnationists believe that the average gap between death and rebirth is eight years.

2. Tal died in 1992.

3. I was born in 2000.

Just sayin'.

I sit on the grassy mound overlooking the chess tables, scanning the boards for a game about to end.

There. I walk over to a table where two middle-aged guys are playing. Black has plenty of time still on the clock but he's a whole rook down. He should have resigned already.

The guy with the white pieces has a tweed jacket, a wispy moustache and a bald spot the size of Brooklyn. He's winning this game, but if his pawn structure is anything to go by (which it is), he's a greater-spotted patzer of the first order. He is taking forever to press home his advantage, but luckily for him his opponent blunders a second rook and resigns.

I take my place on the stone seat in front of Tweed Jacket. 'Wanna play?'

He takes out a chapstick and applies it carefully, staring at me with pale blue eyes. 'Five bucks?'

'Sure.'

And so it begins. We set the clocks to three minutes, shake hands and start to play. Tweed Jacket goes for a Nimzo-Indian, following the book line from memory. He plays like a GM until the thirteenth move and then gets lost.

'Tell me something,' I say. 'Why bother memorizing openings if you don't understand the principles behind them?'

He scowls and pushes a central pawn, slapping his clock violently. My own clock is ticking now, but I just sit back and look at my opponent. 'Did you hear me?' I said. 'Why bother memorizing—'

'Hurry up and move,' he snaps.

My bishop swoops, capturing one of his kingside pawns. 'Check.'

I haven't calculated the sacrifice. A stronger player would recapture in a heartbeat, but Tweed Jacket just stares at it dully like it's a knife in his chest.

I slap my clock to set his ticking. 'Take the bishop,' I tell him.

'Not so fast.'

'Come on, Tweedie,' I say. 'A sacrifice is best refuted by accepting it.'

'Be quiet. Let me think.'

'If you don't take it, you're toast.'

'I'll be the judge of that.'

The more I tell him to take the stupid bishop, the more convinced he is that it's a trap. He's staring at the board and waving his hands to silence me.

Three young guys in sharp suits show up and start watching our game. City slickers on their lunch break.

'Who wants to play the winner?' I ask.

'Me,' says the middle one.

'I hope you've brought your wallet.'

His friends nudge him and cackle.

Tweed Jacket reaches for his king, but instead of capturing the invader he just pushes his king into the corner. I retreat my bishop. I'm a pawn up and Tweedie's kingside is leaking like a stuck hog.

Forty-five seconds later I've won the game. Tweedie hands over five bucks and Sharp Suit takes his place on the stone bench. Nice eyes but too much hair gel.

'I was thinking ten bucks would make it more interesting,' he says.

'Pity. I was going to say a hundred bucks.'

Out of the corner of my eye I see Spencer Fawkes whip his neck around to stare at me.

Sharp Suit is staring too, his face frozen in disbelief. And then he agrees, because his friends are watching and because he's got more money than sense, and because he thinks this gorgeous wig is my actual hair.

Sharp Suit starts off sound enough, but a patzer is a patzer. I smash his face in with a Blackmar-Diemer and mate him in twenty-three moves.

'Miniature,' I whisper.

'What?' The face above the stiff white collar is turning puce.

'A game that takes fewer than twenty-five moves is called a miniature.'

He slams a hundred bucks on the table and walks off, pushing his way angrily through the crowd.

Blitz is not real chess. I'm not gonna pretend it is. It's another game entirely, a crazy, sweaty-toothed game which is less about chess and more about balls and educated guesses. But don't diss it. I've only been here ten minutes and already I'm a hundred and five bucks up. I couldn't earn that in a whole day at Gonuts Donuts.

I play three more guys in quick succession and beat them effortlessly. I'm in the zone now, and the games are playing themselves. I can see so deep into each position, I feel like a god. Flow, that's what Coach used to call it. I'm flowing through the games and the five-dollar bills are flowing into my pocket. It's an antidote to the frustration of Pune, a pressure release after a week without chess, a big fat Welcome Home to the game I never quite stopped loving.

The crowd is buzzing and the challengers are getting harder to beat. Park players are not all deadbeats, and some of the players who sit down opposite me are strong club level. A couple of them might even be masters. I put on a show for the kibitzers, setting up sharp positions where a single tempo can make all the difference between a big win and a crushing fail. I open a few of the games with Giuoco Piano (the 'Quiet Game' – ha!) and then bust the center wide open, making for wild positions that make spectators gasp. I let pieces hang all over the board. I unleash shattering tactical combos – *bam! bam! bam!* – that make my opponents grind their teeth and slap their foreheads like cartoon characters. I offer double or quits to everyone I play, and to the patzers I offer knight odds, rook odds, once even queen odds. I've made a thousand bucks in a couple of hours. *A thousand dollars.* Is this how it feels to be a rock star?

As I give checkmate for the twenty-ninth time, my latest conquest hands over his cash and melts away. Suddenly a waft of cheap eau-de-cologne assails me. Lowering himself onto the stone bench across the board from me is GM Roderick Wilde, a swathe of greasy hair side-combed across his shiny pate. Wilde used to be one of America's top grandmasters but then he had three bad seasons back to back and dropped off the tournament circuit. Now he works as chess columnist for a bunch of newspapers and magazines. *Chess Tales from the Wilde Side,* that sort of thing.

Kit is making a Timeout sign with his hands. *That's enough*, he's trying to say. *Quit while you're ahead.*

Wilde looks at me levelly. His lip curls. 'I've never seen you in the park before,' he says. 'What's your rating?'

'Better than yours.' I gaze back at him without blinking. 'But hey, once a GM always a GM, right? They can't take that away from you.'

Color rises in the GM's cheeks and he laughs a bit too loudly. 'Belligerent little harpy, aren't you? Let's see if I can't take you down a peg or two.' He grabs the white pieces without even asking, and we set up the board. 'Five minutes, fifty bucks,' he says.

We open with a Sicilian Najdorf and I play a novelty on move twelve to get the old man on unfamiliar territory. Wilde's forehead glistens and the reek of cologne gets stronger. He's nervous.

Aside from our own wager, there is a ton of other betting going on. People are leaning over the board waving five- or ten-dollar bills at each other like drinkers at a bar. Wilde is excited by the flurry of money passing hands. On move twenty-six, with the position still equal, he leans over the board and offers to double the stake to a hundred bucks.

'Sure.' I flick my wig hair behind my shoulders. 'Though I'm surprised you can afford it, what with the court case and everything.'

71

'Court case?'

'The plagiarism one.' I smile sweetly and advance my knight. 'Didn't some blogger accuse you of copying your chess columns straight off his blog?'

'That is preposterous!' Roderick Wilde pushes a pawn and slaps the clock irritably. 'There is no such court case. You just made that up.'

The pawn push wasn't the move I was expecting. Aggressive, yes, but somehow premature. It feels like he's handed me an opportunity. I just can't see it yet.

'I love the moment when I crush a man's ego,' says a deep voice suddenly. *'I love the moment when I crush a man's ego.'* I take out my phone and place it on the table next to the board. *'I love the moment when I crush a man's ego,'* repeats Bobby.

'Turn it off,' snaps the grandmaster.

'What's wrong, sir? You never been trash talked by a dead man?' I glance at the number of the incoming call. It's Randal from the donut shop. I'm late for work. 'You mind if I take this call, sir? It's kind of important.'

'I'm not stopping the clocks.'

'I'm not asking you to stop the clocks, sir. Just sit tight and look pretty.'

As I put the phone to my ear, I see shock and amusement written in the faces all around me. In the sudden hush, the ticks of my chess clock sound like hammer blows.

GM Wilde leans back and folds his arms, but his face is ashen. The stakes of this game just went up, and he knows it. If he loses now, he'll be a laughing stock.

Randal is in my ear, saying *Hello Hello* all angry like.

'Hello, boss,' I say. 'Yes, I know why you're calling . . . I know, I'm sorry . . . I'll be with you in ten minutes . . . I'm just crushing a GM.'

What?

'I said, I'm just coming out of the gym.'

Randal's voice in my ear seems like it's coming at me from a million miles away. He jabbers on and on, and all the while I'm gazing deep into the position on the board before me, willing it to give up its secrets. There's something there, I know there is.

'Yeah, boss, I know . . . I know . . . I'll see you soon.' Something stirs at the back of my mind. Something good.

'She's going to lose on time.' Anna's precise Russian accent cuts through the hubbub of kibitzers. 'She's down to thirty seconds. There's no way back from this.'

And then I spot it. It comes to me as if in a dream, a move so utterly beautiful and unexpected that I think my heart is going to stop.

I put down the phone and look at Wilde. 'I'm going to resign,' I say.

'Of course you are,' smirks the grandmaster. 'You've got twenty-five seconds and no attack. Good try, kiddo. You owe me a hundred bucks.' He holds out a flabby hand on the end of a hairless wrist.

I ignore his outstretched hand, move my queen to g3 and slap the clock. 'I wasn't talking about the game, sir. I was talking about my job. I'm going to resign from my job and play chess in the park instead. I like it here.'

GM Wilde stares at me, and then looks down at the board. My queen stands nose to nose with the three pawns that protect his castled king. He can capture my queen in no less than three different ways.

He reaches out to take the piece, then stops, his hand hovering in mid-air. He's spoiled for choice – except he's not. Each way of taking the queen has its own disastrous consequences. I hear a gasp from someone in the crowd, a smothered cuss and a giggle. They get it now. Kibitzers whisper and murmur. Pent-up energy bubbles on the edge of the group like a faraway storm.

My clock is showing twenty-two seconds. That's twenty-two seconds for *all* my remaining moves. I don't think I've ever felt so alive. I have goose bumps on my arms, and I am completely aware of the space my body occupies. I can feel every movement of my heart and lungs, every noise in the crowd, every flap of every pigeon wing, every breath of wind.

The grandmaster chooses the least bad of the three options and taps his clock. I slam a bishop onto h3. This is flow like I've never experienced it before. This is why chess is the greatest game on earth. This is why all of these people from different walks of life will keep on coming to the park until their dying day.

I'm done with calculations. The only question now is, can I move my fingers fast enough to get the win?

A hole has appeared in Wilde's defenses. He's throwing pieces into the hole to avoid checkmate. He gives up his own queen – he has no choice – and then his light-square bishop and a knight. I'm two pieces up and flying.

There's no way the grandmaster is going to resign. Not when I've only got fifteen seconds left on my clock. Fourteen seconds. Thirteen seconds. I move my king into the corner and tap the clock.

He bends forward over the board and links his fingers together across his greasy hairline. Then he thrusts a knight forward to the sixth rank and hits the clock so hard he nearly knocks it off the table. This is desperate stuff from Wilde. He's ignoring my passed pawn and relying on his knight to deliver a few surprise checks and run my time down.

I push the passed pawn. Nine seconds.

In comes that pesky knight. Check.

I move my king.

Check again, and the knight falls.

'What you got now, fish?' I'm talking like Nathan Banks, I can't help it. 'Come on, fish, what you got?'

He moves a bishop to threaten my passed pawn. I move a rook, he takes the pawn, I take the bishop. Six seconds left on my clock, and his exposed king is off and running like a ferret in a forest fire.

I push another pawn to clear the way. He takes it. Five seconds left.

I line up my rooks. Four seconds left.

Check. Three.

Check. Two.

Checkmate. I've won.

I stop the clocks and the crowd erupts around me. A woolen hat flies through the air. Someone behind me is shaking me by the shoulders. Little Nathan Banks is leaping around like a mad thing. 'Did you SEE that?' he yells. 'Did you SEE how fast her hands were movin'? She's a FREAK!'

Wilde is staring at the clock. He has more than a minute left, and I have half a second.

I hold my hand out to the grandmaster, but he pretends not to see it. He gets unsteadily to his feet, counts five twenties onto the board and stumbles away.

The crowd is still cheering and clapping, so I hop up onto the table and take a semi-ironic bow.

And you know what? I haven't felt this happy in YEARS.

I RESIGN

I walk into Gonuts Donuts like I'm in a dream.

Ronda doesn't recognize me at first. 'Good day, ma'am, how can I WOAH—'

'Hey, Ronda. Where's the boss?'

'In the office,' says Ronda. 'What happened to your hair?'

'It's a wig. Like it?' I hop up onto a stool and help myself to a donut.

Ronda stares. 'You can't sit there. You can't eat that.'

'Don't worry, I'll pay.'

'What's wrong with you, Leah?' Ronda's hands are on her hips.

I grin at her like a loon. 'I've got a secret to tell you.'

'What?'

'I play chess.'

'That's your secret?'

'Yeah. But here's the thing, I play chess *really* well.'

'Okaaay.'

'I'm one of the best young players in the world.'

'Wow.'

'And I tried to give up, but it didn't work. Cos if I don't play, I'll die.'

'You'll die?'

'Yes.'

'I get it.' Ronda smiles and blinks. 'I used to feel that way about Candy Crush.'

I dust donut sugar off my hands and jump down from the stool. 'I need to talk to your dad.'

Suddenly Ronda is a blur of flying hair and flapping hands.

'Hold on, Leah, you can't go in there like that. You know the rules about clothes and makeup. Hey!'

She's right, I do know the rules. Gonuts Donuts crew have to be plain and wholesome and girl-next-door. But the fact is, even the people who live next door to me don't think of me as girl-next-door.

I'm still intoxicated from playing chess in the park. From feeling the smooth wooden pieces under my fingers, the sun on my back, dollars against my thighs and pure fiery genius crackling through my veins. So if Randal or Ronda or anyone else thinks I'm going to go from badass wig-wearing celeb-smashing chess sensation to coffee-pouring girl-next-door, they've got another think coming.

I walk into the admin office. Randal is sitting at his desk, impaling invoices on a metal spike.

'Hello, boss.'

'Seventeen minutes late,' he says, not looking up.

'I just wanted to—'

'Seventeen minutes!' he snaps. 'So how 'bout a little less *hello boss*-ing and a little more *sorry boss*-ing.'

'Sorry, boss.'

He grabs another invoice, glances up at me and notices my wig. The invoice misses the spike completely and the side of

Randal's hand slams down right on top of it. A yowl of pain echoes off the bare walls and filing cabinets. The boss is off his chair and hopping around, hugging his hand to his chest.

'You are KIDDING me!' he yells, and then he lurches right up close and wags a blood-stained finger in my face. 'This is a respectable baked goods establishment. What makes you think you can drift in seventeen minutes late dressed like a ten-dollar hooker?'

'I wanted to tell you in person, that's all.'

'Tell me what?'

'I quit.'

'What? Who the—? No you don't, missy! I took a chance on you! I trained you up from nothing! Hey, come back here! I'm not done with you.'

I walk out of the office, smack into Ronda who's listening at the door.

'Leah,' she squeaks.

'I'm sorry,' I tell her. 'Here's some money for that donut.'

I thrust ten bucks into her hand and hurry along the corridor into the fluorescent glare of the shop. The customers are all gawking at me and one girl has her hand over her mouth, like she's never heard an argument before.

Randal pursues me, cradling his injured hand. There's blood on his shirt front and his cuffs, but he doesn't seem to notice. 'I know your sort!' he yells. 'Spineless, that's what you are!'

I open the door and turn to wave goodbye to the Gonuts Donuts clientele.

'This is not happening!' Randal yells. 'You don't get to quit. You are fired, do you hear me? Axed. Canned. Pink slipped. Decruited. Tossed out on your big cahuna!'

I glide out into the humid afternoon, and the rage of the donut chief fades to distant thunder behind me.

Gonuts Donuts. Figures.

SCABBERWOCKY

I cross over 8th Street and sit on a cast-iron bench. I know I've made the right choice, but the heat of Randal's anger took me by surprise, and my heart is pounding like a brick in a dryer.

Kit appears out of nowhere. He plonks himself down beside me and lolls an arm over the back of the bench. His fingertips are near my shoulder.

'Don't touch me,' I warn him.

'Wouldn't dream of it.'

Kit's voice sounds strange. Probably something to do with the purple bruise on his jaw. We sit in silence for a minute or two, then he puffs out his cheeks noisily.

'Queen g3,' he says. 'Magnificent.'

'I know, right?' I crack a smile. 'You could go a whole lifetime of chess without playing a move like that. It's just a pity no one will ever know it happened.'

'Except for fifty deadbeats in the park.'

'Exactly.'

'And a few million on YouTube.'

I look up at him. 'Are you serious? Was someone filming?'

'Apparently, yes. Some guy called Scabberwocky uploaded the whole thing to YouTube. People are calling you "Park Girl", and the great minds on the chess.com forums have temporarily suspended their arguments about Borislav Ivanov's shoes in order to address the question of your real identity.'

'Sheesh. How many hits has the video got so far?'

Kit takes out his phone and refreshes the browser. 'Just over four thousand. Not bad, when you consider it was only uploaded twenty-two minutes ago. By the end of the day, I'm guessing a hundred thousand views. A week from now, the sky's the limit. And you can wipe that smile off your face,

Leah Baxter. This is a serious breach for the Poisoned Pawns. If we wanted our games on YouTube, we'd film them ourselves.'

He's right, of course. Chess hustling is classified as public gambling, which is contravened in the New York Penal Code.

'Does Scabberwocky's video show any money changing hands?' I ask.

'Clear as day.' Kit puts his phone back in his pocket. 'So if the NYPD's finest want a break from investigating stabbings and shootings and Grand Larceny in the Fourth Degree, they could very well turn their attentions to your queen g3 mischief.'

A pigeon flies down onto the back of the bench behind me, making me jump. I flap my hand to shoo it away.

'What's done is done,' says Kit. 'And I've got to admit, as a piece of viral content that video has pretty much everything. Chauvinistic old man outwitted by super-intelligent girl who also happens to be ballsy and borderline cute.'

'Borderline?'

'It's amazing what a good wig can do for a girl.'

'Very funny.' I pull off the red wig and shove it into Mom's purse. A passer-by on the sidewalk startles and glances back at me in horror like I've taken out an eyeball or something. 'I'm going home,' I say.

Kit jumps to his feet. 'Walk you to the subway?'

'Sure.'

We walk in silence along 8th Street, heading west. Number 1 5th Avenue looms above us, its false shadows and turret-like corners giving it the look of an enormous art deco rook. Reminds me of a chess set I saw in the Thompson Street chess shop one time: Empire State Buildings for queens, Chrysler Buildings for bishops, brownstone townhouses for pawns. What were the knights? I rack my brains, trying to remember.

'Join us, Leah,' says Kit suddenly. 'We'll be the best hustlers the city has ever seen.'

'Why shouldn't I hustle on my own? I'd earn a fortune.'

'Yes, you would. But I warn you, the park is not always a nice place to be in. It's good to have friends to watch your back.'

Get some friends. That was number four on my Plan to Reinvent Myself, right under *Get a tattoo.* And look how that worked out.

I feel another sudden surge of resentment about the whole tattoo thing, so I side eye the bruise on Kit's jaw to cheer me up. We turn left at the lights and walk through the triumphal arch into the park. Dozens of students are arrayed on the plaza steps like baboons on a rock, watching other baboons go by.

'Take your time,' Kit says. 'Ask yourself what you really want.'

That's easy. Dad not to be dead. Mom to quit bugging me. Adrenalin. Oblivion.

'All right, I'm in,' I say.

'Yes!' Kit punches the air.

'But no dead weight,' I say. 'If I'm in, Spencer Fawkes is out.'

'Sure. I'll call him tonight.'

We stroll along the northside footpath, out of the park at Hangman's Elm, then down 6th Avenue toward the subway.

'Pillow fight in the park tomorrow,' says Kit. Then, seeing my blank expression, 'It happens every year. Hundreds of people in crazy costumes, bashing each other with pillows. We could go together if you wanted a break from chess.'

'I already had a break from chess. Break's over.'

'Okay,' says Kit. 'In that case, I'll see you here at nine tomorrow. And don't forget the wig.'

I skitter down the subway steps two at a time. At the turnstile I dig into Mom's purse for my ticket and my fingers close around a piece of paper. It's Mick's drawing of a dead white king with a dazzling phoenix rising out of it.

I'm still sore about that phoenix, but as I look down at it, I can't help smiling. I'm going to be the best chess hustler New York has ever seen. I'll take on every patzer, wannabe and has-been in the city, and I'll smash them one by one at twenty bucks a throw.

MAHLER

The first thing I hear when I open the front door back home is a deep male voice coming from the kitchen to my left.

Dad!

My heart leaps, then sinks, that familiar jolt of remembrance. Dead men don't talk.

It's Coach. He's in the kitchen, arguing with Mom.

'I was going to go there!' cries Mom.

'Too bad!' snorts Coach.

I hear a scraping of chairs and a stifled giggle. They're not arguing. They're flirting.

I tiptoe past the kitchen door, along the corridor and into my room. It's been a while since I last mistook Coach's voice for Dad's, and it's got me rattled. I'm squeezing the skin between my thumb and fingers and shaking like a spider on speed.

What is Coach doing here, anyway? He knows I've given up chess. Doesn't he have work to do? Who does he think he is, coming to our house to gossip and laugh and stop my heart?

I close my bedroom door and grab the bottle of Clubman aftershave off my dressing table. I unscrew the cap, lift it to my nose and breathe in Dad's musky, slightly citric scent. The line drawing on the front of the bottle shows a man in a top hat and smoking jacket.

I remember a few times watching Dad patting this aftershave on his cheeks at the bathroom mirror. One time he saw me in the doorway there and he tried to do a Charlie Chaplin heel-click for me. Banged his knee on the sink and fell over sideways, cussing like a sailor.

How old was I when that happened? Four? Seven? I have no idea.

I inhale the scent once more, then replace the bottle on the dresser. Right this second I would sell my soul for just one hug from my dad. Or to tell him about the Wilde game and hear him laugh.

Music, that's what I need. I fumble with my phone, trying and failing to dock it on the speakers. When at last it clicks into place, I select Mahler's Second Symphony, *The Resurrection*, and wait for the music to start.

Here it comes at last, the slow calming march of basses and cellos. Dad loved this symphony.

I take off Mom's skirt and jacket and throw on some jeans and a cable-knit sweater. An oboe twitters above the funeral march, and then a cacophony of wild French horns, chilling and sardonic.

I lift Anatoly out of his cage, drape him across my shoulders and sit down on my bed to look at my phone. Anatoly slithers around my neck, his caress as whisper-light as a feather boa.

The Park Girl video is easy to find. It's got over a hundred thousand views already and the hashtags #egocrush, #GMWilde and #thuglifechess are all over the internet. The game has made the front page of chess.com and even a bunch of clickbait sites. ARROGANT GRANDMASTER TELLS TEEN HE'S GOING TO TAKE HER DOWN A PEG OR TWO. YOU WON'T BELIEVE WHAT HAPPENS NEXT.

I guess Roderick Wilde can kiss goodbye to his career in chess journalism. This video will finish him. He'll write a few column inches about the experience of losing to me, and after that no one will take him seriously ever again.

Anatoly slides down into my lap and coils himself into a ball. I rub his scaly skin and watch the view count on the video rise. *The Resurrection* lurches into a series of wild death throes and finally collapses to a single drawn-out C. My heart swells with awe and sadness as the note fades into silence.

Right, that's it. I'm going in.

With Anatoly around my neck I tiptoe along the corridor toward the kitchen. Mom and Coach are sitting at the table in front of a bowl of beef jerky and a Scrabble board.

Scrabble! I've never seen Coach play anything but chess. Demeaning, that's what it is.

As I stand there watching, Mom reaches over and grabs one of Coach's tiles. He slaps her hand. She squawks and giggles.

Anatoly hisses suddenly and Mom and Coach look up, startled.

'Hi, honey,' says Mom. 'I didn't hear you come in.' She sits bolt upright and smiles brightly.

First time Mom ever called me *honey*. Stop the clocks. Write it in the history books.

'Hey, Mom,' I say. 'Hey, Coach. What are you doing here?'

'I was in the area,' he says. 'Thought I'd drop by and see you both. See if you've reconsid—'

'I haven't.'

'That's too bad. I never had you down as a quitter.'

There it is again, the q word. In the silence that follows I scan the Scrabble board upside-down. RAVES. ICIER. OBEISANT. The kitchen units are closing in on me. HOVER.

UPDATES. PANSY. The ceiling is pressing down. HOPE. SPEW. SHADOW.

Coach eyes Anatoly warily. 'You got a snake,' he says. 'Awesome.'

'Leah and Anatoly are the best of friends,' says Mom. 'I'll admit, I had some concerns about having a snake in the house, but look at him now. He's ever so affectionate.'

'He's not affectionate,' I say. 'It may look like affection but in reality he's just sponging body warmth.' I look at Coach pointedly. He shifts in his seat.

Another silence, even longer than the last. Coach picks up a Scrabble tile and gazes at it imploringly.

'Since you're here, Leah,' he says at last, 'tell your mother that ZEN is a perfectly good Scrabble word.'

'Is not!' laughs Mom, stabbing the air with her index finger.

'Is so,' says Coach. 'The adjectival form has a small z.'

I fix myself a bowl of cereal, pouring the milk so fast that it sloshes over the worktop.

'There *is* no adjectival form,' Mom insists. 'Isn't that right, Leah?'

'I honestly don't know,' I mutter, and all I want is to get back to my room to drown in Mahler and write my blog.

GRIND

Last night I dreamed about Dad. I dreamed we'd pitched a tent by a lake and were taking turns to skim stones on the water.

I hate waking up from happy dreams about Dad. It's the same every time, the sudden heart-stopping remembrance that feels like falling off a cliff. And today it's even worse because I just found a letter lying on the doormat addressed to Mr Jack Baxter – junk mail from some dumbass travel agency.

I open the envelope with trembling fingers.

Dear Mr Baxter, the letter begins. *Do you secretly long to escape the 9 to 5 grind?*

FEAR NO ONE

Kit meets me outside the subway at 9 o'clock, as planned. He is pale and breathless. 'Boy, am I glad to see you!' he says. 'Guess how many people have turned up at the tables today? Over a hundred, that's how many. And the Park Girl video? Nine hundred thousand views!'

We walk up Waverly Place toward the park.

'Did you dump Spencer?' I ask.

'Yes,' says Kit. 'And no, he didn't take it well.'

Through the iron railings I see a line of men and boys in front of an empty chess table. The line snakes all over the arena, up the grassy bank and down again. Every single one of them is going to die one day and not one of them has any awareness of it.

'I got you a present,' says Kit. 'My way of saying thank you for joining the syndicate.' He hands me a small package wrapped in brown paper.

'What is it?'

'Open it and see, dummy.'

I unwrap the paper and out slips a book, a compact leather-bound volume with bright gold lettering along the spine: RESHEVSKY ON CHESS. I open it carefully. It's a 1948 first edition, signed by the great Samuel Reshevsky himself.

'It's beautiful,' I whisper.

Kit smiles happily. 'Turn to page three of the introduction,' he says. 'Second paragraph.'

I turn the pages and read aloud. ' *"My strength consists of a fighting spirit, a great desire to win, and a stubborn defense whenever in trouble. I rarely become discouraged in an inferior situation, and I fear no one."* '

'*Fear no one.*' Kit's wonky eyes twinkle. 'I read that and thought of you.'

'Thank you.' I put the book in my bag and stand there awkwardly for an age, wondering whether I should hug him or not. Don't want to give him the wrong idea. At last I stick out my right hand for a handshake.

Kit bends down, takes the proffered hand and kisses it like he thinks he's Sir Walter Raleigh. Although it's more of a mime, really. Doesn't actually make contact.

'Line's getting longer,' I say. 'I should go.'

'Sure.' Kit lets go of my hand. 'Keep your head down and take each game as it comes. I'll be beside you the whole time.'

'Play your own games,' I tell him. 'I can look after myself.'

PERISCOPE

I dig my nails into my palms and march through the southwest arch into the crowded arena, tossing my long red wig hair over my shoulders.

'Park Girl!' cries a young boy, and the next thing I know, I'm being rushed by patzers with sharpies and selfie sticks.

'No autographs,' I tell them. 'If you're here to play, stick around. If not, get lost.'

I take my place on the cold stone bench. I have the last table in the row, same as yesterday, and the pieces are already set up.

'Chess! Chess! Chess!' chant the crowd.

My first opponent looks about my age. Twinkly blue eyes, smooth skin, shampoo-commercial hair. Video camera strapped on his head.

'I'm Seb Giles,' says the boy, and he looks at me like he expects me to recognize him. 'YouTube Live,' he adds. 'I promised my followers I'd broadcast my game with you.'

I crane my neck to look for Kit but he's already engrossed in a game. I guess he took me at my word when I told him I didn't need his help. I think for a second or two and decide I'm fine with this Seb kid filming me. That horse already bolted.

'Twenty-dollar stake,' I tell him. 'Plus fifty if you want to film.' I hide a pawn in each fist and hold them out for him to choose.

'Greetings!' Seb cries. 'And welcome to a brand-new Geekquest adventure. I'm Seb Giles and today I'm here with the YouTube chess phenomenon Park Girl. Some of you heard me talk about her in last night's show and this morning we're together in Washington Square Park, scene of yesterday's epic game. Don't be fooled by those cute dimples or those soulful brown eyes, my friends, there's a brain the size of a planet lurking beh—'

'Get on with it.' I snap. 'Choose a hand.'

He taps my left hand. Black. I start the clocks and play e4.

'I'm challenging Park Girl to a game of bullet chess,' jabbers Seb. 'If you're as excited as I am for this titanic battle, go ahead and mash that heart button. And don't forget to subscribe!'

'Make your move.'

He pushes his g pawn two squares. 'What should I call you, sweetheart?'

'Park Girl.' I push a central pawn. 'And if you call me sweetheart again I'll rip your grin off and feed it to the pigeons.'

'What did I tell you, folks? Cute as a button and hard as nails.' Still chuckling, he pushes his f pawn one square forward. Literally the worst thing he could have done.

I slide my queen to h4. Checkmate.

'Noooooool' Seb leaps up, whips the camera off his head and pans it around. He films the crowd hooting and hollering behind him. He films himself, eyes popping, tongue lolling. He films me setting up the pieces for the next game. I can feel my nostrils twitching as I struggle not to smile. The Fool's Mate was deliberate, of course. You have to know what you're doing to lose that quick.

Seb milks the moment for all its worth, then reaches over and slaps seventy bucks on the table in front of me. He knows the video will earn him ten times that amount by the end of the day.

'Thanks for the game,' he says. 'How was it for you?'

'Disappointing.'

The YouTuber disappears into the crowd, babbling blithely to his followers.

'Who's next?' I say.

A giant of a man sits down opposite me and says good morning in a very high-pitched voice. The halfwits at the back of the line burst out laughing. They'd laugh at anything, the mood they're in.

I've got White again. I play a simple Queen's Gambit and slay the giant in twenty moves. He pays his dues and lumbers off.

'Chess! Chess! Chess!' chant the crowd.

'I'm next,' says a husky voice, 'but I don't have twenty bucks to lose.'

I look up from the board. Standing in front of me is a teenage boy. Dark hair, dark eyes, neck muscles like a bull terrier.

'Really, jock? You want to play me for free? You think I come here for the joy of the beautiful game?'

'Okay, forget about playing,' he says. 'Can we just talk?'

'Talk? Are you for real?'

'My name is Travis. I need advice about how to improve my chess. I've got to gain two hundred rating points real fast.'

'And if you don't, the bad guys will kill your dog, right?'

A muscle twitches in his jaw. 'You making fun of me?'

'It depends. What's your rating?'

'Sixteen hundred.'

'Yes, I'm making fun of you. But there's a line of other people behind you, all waiting to be made fun of, and those people have money, so . . .'

Travis leans over the chessboard and lowers his voice. 'I'll be your bodyguard,' he says.

'Excuse me?'

'You're a hustler,' he says, 'which means you're a magnet for trouble. I'll keep you safe and in return you get me to eighteen hundred rating points.'

'Move along, knucklehead,' shouts someone further back in the line. 'Stop wasting our time.'

Travis ignores the taunt. 'Think about it,' he whispers. 'A few chess lessons in exchange for peace of mind.'

'Peace of mind?' I snort. 'It's been so long, I wouldn't even know what to do with peace of mind.'

'Advice, then,' he pleads. 'Recommend a book. Anything.'

He looks so earnest, I actually feel sorry for him. '*My 60 Memorable Games* by Bobby Fischer,' I tell him. 'Study one game a day on an empty stomach, and in two months you'll rank eighteen hundred.'

'Thanks.'

'Now beat it. I've got work to do.'

FEDS

At eleven o'clock in the morning the party comes to an abrupt halt, which is a pity because I'm in the middle of a half-decent game. My opponent has dug himself in behind a Berlin Stonewall and I'm throwing my kingside pawns forward trying to bash a way through. Just as we are reaching the crucial moment, my opponent jumps up from the board and runs away.

Amazed, I watch him go. I've had plenty of people rage-quit in the middle of a game, but they usually just knock over their king and leave. They don't leap up and sprint off like a fox with its tail on fire. Besides, the position was still sharp. Possibilities on both sides.

Then it dawns on me. The halfwits at the back of the crowd are no longer chanting 'Chess! Chess! Chess!' but 'Feds! Feds! Feds!' Three police officers – two men and one woman – are pushing their way through the crowd toward the chess tables.

'Nobody move!' shouts an officer. 'Everybody stay right where you are!'

Like that's going to happen. The tables are emptying faster than a patzer's pockets.

The policeman glances down at something in his hand, then points at me. 'You!' he shouts. 'Don't move a muscle.'

For a blitz player, I've been slow off the mark. But now that I've assessed my options, not moving a muscle seems like a bad idea. I vault over the back of the stone bench and set off running across the grass.

Too late, I realize I've left the Samuel Reshevsky book on the chess table. I can't believe I did that. It must have cost Kit a fortune and I was so looking forward to adding it to my gasoline-soaked collection. For a moment I consider going back for it, but one glance behind me tells me that's impossible. There are two police officers right on my tail.

Anna is just ahead of me, running toward the center of the park with long ungainly strides, her elbows pumping, her blonde ponytail swishing from side to side.

Two more officers are closing in on us from the sides. 'Stop right there, both of you!' they yell.

I speed up. My front foot catches Anna's heel and down she goes, sprawling on the grass. I jump over her flailing limbs and keep running. She screams at me in Russian.

I head north on the wide concrete path, weaving among moms with strollers, and rollerbladers, joggers and junkies. The pigeon man is sitting on his usual bench, his head and shoulders covered in birds. Students loll on the grass in the April sun. A street performer is juggling floppy hats. He drops one as I fly past.

There is a commotion near the north gate. Shouting, screaming and laughter.

I'd completely forgotten. Today is the day of the mass pillow fight.

There are at least three police officers on my tail. One is speaking into her radio, relaying my position to unseen hunters. The mating net is closing around me. Time to add complexity.

I veer toward the brawl and dive into the middle of the pillow-flinging throng. In the blizzard of flying feathers, a pillow flollops me full in the face. I gasp and struggle on.

Some of the pillow bearers have come in fancy dress. As I press further into the crowd, I am surrounded by superheroes, animals, pirates and a whole bunch of Where's Waldos. A pillow hits me on the back, another on the side of my head. A velociraptor appears in front of me and deals another swinging blow.

I tackle the dinosaur around the waist. Down she goes, and now I'm lying on top of the velociraptor while a chef and a cowboy whack my back and legs. It's b to the power of izarre, and that's the truth.

'Get off me!' groans the velociraptor.

'Listen, pea brain,' I whisper. 'I'll give you fifty dollars for the pillow and the dino-head. Five seconds to decide.'

Turns out one second is all she needs. I press the bills into her hand, rip off the wig, put on the dino head, stagger to my feet and make my way through the mêlée, swinging my pillow in front of me to carve a path.

'Stop! Police!' cries a voice at my right hand. A chubby police officer is doubled over, shielding his head from a rain of soft but persistent blows. He's not talking to me but to his assailants. 'Stop,' he squawks. 'I'm a police officer. This is not a costume.'

A photo lies on the ground next to the hapless policeman. It's a grainy still from a surveillance camera, a girl in a red wig sitting at a chess table.

I was right. It was me they wanted.

'Quick, Leah, come with me,' a boy whispers in my ear. With my dino-head tunnel vision it takes a moment for me to see him, but when I do, I feel momentarily scared. He's wearing jeans, hoodie, gray Reeboks and one of those *Anonymous* masks with the thin vertical beard and the sinister grin.

'Don't look so shocked,' he laughs, taking hold of my arm. 'Kit sent me to get you. Come on, this place is swarming with Feds.'

We slip away from the pillow fight, past the George Washington monument and through the triumphal arch onto Washington Square North. My dino head stinks of cheap hairspray. I can't wait to take it off.

My rescuer walks close beside me, his grip tightening on my upper arm. He steers me across the crosswalk and up 5th Avenue, past the nail salon, Patrick's Bar and the Irish fortune teller's shop.

'Who are you?' I ask.

'Can't you guess?' he says. 'Mask's a clue.'

'Tell me right now or I'm going.'

Anonymous just laughs.

I try to wrest my arm away, but he redoubles his grip and pulls me sharp left, dragging me up some steps and through an automatic door. Through the eyeholes of my mask I see fluorescent lights, gleaming tiles, crackheads and police officers.

Too late, I remember. The moustache and thin beard of the Anonymous mask are styled on a real historical character. Guy Fawkes.

'Delivery,' my captor calls. 'Leah "Park Girl" Baxter, like I promised.'

An officer hurries out from behind a desk, handcuffs at the ready. 'Thank you, Mr Fawkes. We'll take it from here.'

The boy takes off his mask, and there he is. Spencer Fawkes, leering at me triumphantly.

PRECINCT 12

I guess Spencer's ego could not cope with being dumped from the syndicate. I guess this is revenge. He floats out of that police precinct as free as a kite and I get locked up for contravention of New York's gambling laws on only my second day of hustling. Like the rest of my life, it's not exactly fair.

My holding cell is closet-sized and reeks of sick. I have a bench, an open toilet and one very angry cellmate. Anna Anaconda.

As soon as she sees me, she starts screaming like a bobcat, ludicrous insults direct from her native Russian. She calls me a twisted belly button, an eater of fish stew, a lugger of noodles. She seems to think I tripped her up deliberately and that she would have got away if it wasn't for me.

'*Voron voronu glaz ne vyklyuyet,*' I tell her, remembering one of my Russian proverbs. 'A raven does not peck out the eye of another raven.'

Anna stops dead. 'You speak Russian?'

'I had a Russian boyfriend once.'

'So you know the phrase *moralny erod*?'

'No.'

'It means a moral moron. Someone whose moral sense is twisted or totally non-existent.'

'Oh.'

'Someone with no honor. Someone who would stab her own sister for a fox-fur hat.'

'I didn't mean to trip you, Anna.'

'If I can't play chess I can't pay my college fees. Don't ever speak to me again.'

She sits on the bench and I sit cross-legged on the floor. I close my eyes, calm my pulse and summon up that unfinished Berlin Stonewall game. I can feel Anna's hostile glare boring into me, but I keep focussing on my breathing and on the position in my mind. I try out a dozen possible lines, probing the position for a clear advantage.

Two hours later, a policewoman opens the door and tells us we're going to the Tombs. A chill goes right down through my body. The Tombs are Manhattan's underground holding cells, where natural light and birdsong never penetrate and where felons gnash their teeth while they wait for their arraignment hearings.

Anna folds her arms. 'I want an attorney,' she says.

'The court will assign you one in due course.'

The policewoman cuffs us and takes us to a waiting van. The wire cage inside the van contains Kit and three kibitzers who got caught placing bets. *Kit and the Kibitzers*, like some lame-ass band.

I sit down next to Kit on the hard bench. 'Guess I should have stuck with glazing donuts.'

'Sorry,' says Kit. 'I've never seen them put so many officers on a chess sting.'

Anna laughs bitterly. 'I wonder why they did that. It's not like we did anything to provoke them, is it? Only a million people watched that Park Girl video, right?'

'Calm down,' says Kit. 'Whatever they fine us, we'll earn it back at the tables on Monday.'

'Monday!' Anna spits. 'You think we'll be back at the tables on Monday, like nothing happened? Are you really that stupid?'

With lights flashing and sirens blaring, our van careers down Lafayette Street toward Columbus Park. It shrieks to a stop outside Central Booking and our arresting officer opens the doors to let us out.

Two dark towers rise above us. Just looking at them makes me feel sick and dizzy. My heart is racing. My vision is blurred. My brain is filling up fast with dozens of competing thoughts.

'Hang in there, Leah,' whispers Kit. 'If you can beat Roderick Wilde you can beat Central Booking. Stay close to me and do what I do.'

THE TOMBS

Our arresting officer escorts us through a narrow courtyard between the towers, through an armored booth and into a dingy waiting area that reeks of urine. In the middle of a horseshoe of holding cells is a processing desk manned by three Corrections Officers.

A female officer searches me roughly and confiscates my cash and phone. She slides the shoelaces out of my shoes and the belt out of my jeans. Another officer asks my name, age and address and types them into the computer. Hunt, peck, hunt, peck, you'd think he'd never seen a keyboard before.

Officer Hunt-Peck explains that the law in New York City treats seventeen-year-olds as adults. If I want my mom to be present at my arraignment hearing, they can get in touch with her, but she doesn't have to be here.

Ha. The less Mom knows about this, the better. She thinks I'm wiping counters at Gonuts Donuts this afternoon, and that suits me just fine.

More waiting, more processing: mug shot, retina, fingerprints. For some reason my fingerprint scan takes forever and the CO keeps having to redo it.

'What did you do, Leah?' laughs Kit. 'Burn off your fingerprints with a cigarette?'

The Corrections Officer gives Kit a long malevolent stare. 'Goof off all you like, kid. When you're down in the Tombs and your paperwork gets lost, you'll at least have the memory of your own wit to keep you going.'

The female CO reappears with a bunch of female cons, all handcuffed together in a petulant line of tattoos, tank tops, sneakers and scowls. She cuffs me and Anna to the front of the line and shoves us forward.

'Move it!' she barks.

I feel disembodied, like I'm hovering above myself, looking down. I watch a line of cons shuffle through a maze of dingy corridors and down a flight of steps into a low-ceilinged basement, struggling to walk in their laceless shoes. I watch them waddling clown-like along another corridor. I watch the CO usher them into a large holding cell and uncuff them.

'Welcome to the Tombs,' she says. 'We have the right to hold you here for up to seventy-two hours.'

She marches out, locks the door and leaves.

Seventy-two hours! That's three days and three nights. I should have got them to call my mom after all.

The holding room is thirty-feet long and twenty wide. Ten women sit on metal benches around the sides of the cell. Some of them look up at the newcomers, most stare straight ahead. We newbies stand underneath the fluorescent lights, blinking and rubbing our wrists.

'Hey!' yells Anna. 'I want an attorney!'

No answer, just the clicking of leather heels up the steps away from us.

I sit down on the edge of a bench and take a deep breath. Anna goes over to a brown payphone on the far wall of the cell and lifts the receiver.

'Phone doesn't work, baby,' says a bright-eyed woman in denim dungarees. 'Never has, never will.'

Anna cusses in Russian and slams the phone back into its cradle. 'Officer!' she screams. 'I want an attorney!' She rushes across the cell and flings herself against the bars. But the officer is long gone.

'Take it easy, baby,' drawls Dungarees. 'Right now the Land of the Free is twenty yards above your head. This down here? This is the Land of Shut Up and Submit. You'll get an attorney soon enough, but if you holler like that, they'll keep you here all night long. If you're still here tomorrow morning you'll be needing to use the Comfort Station and there ain't NOBODY wants to do that.' The woman cackles and juts her chin toward the overflowing toilet in the corner.

Anna screws up her face and turns away.

'It won't be nowhere near seventy-two hours,' adds Dungarees. 'They just say that to freak you out.'

I pat the space on the bench beside me, inviting Anna to sit down. You would think she'd be grateful to have friends in a place like this, but haters gonna hate. She plonks herself down twenty feet away on the other side of the cell, scowling like a punk.

Over in the far corner of the cell a lank-haired blonde crouches on the metal bench. Her head is against the wall and her knees are drawn up to her chest. Deep in some private hell of drug withdrawal, she gulps and sweats like a pregnant trout.

Dungarees tugs my sleeve. 'This your first time, baby?' she drawls.

'Yeah.' I pull my arm away.

'What you in for?'

'Chess.'

'Using or dealing?'

'What?'

'The ket. Were you using or dealing?'

'Not ket. Chess.'

'The board game?'

'Yes.'

Dungarees throws back her head and cackles long and loud. 'White girl says she's in for chess,' she announces to the rest of the holding cell. 'I thought she said *ket*!'

General laughter. Best joke these cons have ever heard. A woman in leather trousers slaps her thigh so hard it echoes from wall to wall like a thunderclap.

'I thought you said ket,' repeats Dungarees, wiping her eyes. Then she reaches over and puts a hand on my knee. 'I'm Dora,' she says.

'Leah,' I say.

'Wanna know what I'm in here for, Leah?'

'Sure.'

'Backgammon.'

'Really?'

'No. Credit card fraud.' Her eyes twinkle. 'But I'm innocent, see?'

'Right.'

Dora points at a stocky Hispanic girl in a black leather jacket and pigtails. 'Guess what Carmen over there is in for.'

'I don't know.'

'Bashed her boyfriend's brains out with a fire extinguisher.'

Carmen scowls. 'He had it coming,' she mutters.

FRIC

The two most common questions you get in the Tombs are: 'This your first time?' and: 'What you in for?' Now that Dora has broken the ice, we are all opening up to each other like old-timers, comparing crimes and arrest stories. Most of the women here are accused of larceny, theft, fraud, prostitution or drug possession. Plus two college girls who somehow got themselves arrested for singing in the subway. Everyone except Carmen claims to be innocent.

I am something of a celeb down here, not only because of the chess thing but also for resisting arrest. I tell my cellmates about the pillow fight and the velociraptor disguise. And yes, I exaggerate the story a little because I like their uninhibited laughter and want more of it.

Anna stares at me with undisguised hatred while I tell my tale. When I finish, she gets up and says, 'Who wants to hear a Russian story?'

Everyone does, of course, so Anna starts telling this dumbass joke about two hikers and a bear.

'Anya and Luba are chopping wood in the forest when a grizzly bear jumps out from behind a tree. Luba bends down and starts putting on her running shoes. "What are you doing?" says Anya. "You can't outrun a grizzly bear." Luba replies, "I don't need to outrun the grizzly bear. I just need to outrun you."'

A few of the women laugh and the one in leather trousers slaps her thigh again.

Anna scowls at me. 'What do you think, *Moralny Erod*?' she calls. 'Do you like this Russian story?'

'Drop it,' I say.

Nobody in here cares about our squabble. Dora is already on her feet telling a joke about an alligator in a sperm bank, and soon all the cons are chuckling and groaning and grossing out.

No. Not all of them are chuckling. The junkie in the corner is still in a world of her own, her empty eyes staring out between two curtains of lank hair. As I watch her I realize we're the same, me and her. Both in withdrawal. Both aching for something or someone that has been taken away from us.

'Lunch!' calls a bored female voice, and a tray of sandwiches appears. This time the officer doesn't even come into the cell – just shoves the limp cardboard sandwich boxes and bottles of water through the bars like it's feeding time at the zoo.

If anything could dampen our spirits, it's this curling bread with its mysterious dark brown filling. Dora takes one bite and flings it down in disgust. The junkie in the corner, my soul sister, climbs onto the bench and starts smearing the dark brown paste across the peeling walls. No one speaks as she works on her mural: a towering stick woman with dots all down her cheeks.

I close my eyes and try lying down on the bench, but the metal is so slippery I keep sliding off. And I keep patting my pocket wondering where my phone is, only to remember that it's been confiscated.

Minutes pass.

'I challenge you,' says a voice.

I sit up and open my eyes. Carmen the fire extinguisher killer is standing over me, and in her cupped hands she holds a mound of confetti made from torn-up sandwich boxes. Looking closer, I see she's made different shapes: squares, circles, crowns, towers and horses. A home-made chess set.

'My daddy taught me,' she says. 'Come on, white girl, let's play.'

'No thanks.'

'You got something better to do?' Her tone is more aggressive than shy this time.

'What's your rating?' I ask her.

'What do you mean, rating?'

She doesn't have a rating. She doesn't even know what a rating is. And she wants to play me at chess. Ha!

'One game,' I say wearily. 'You be White.'

We sit cross-legged on the checkered floor tiles, cordon off sixty-four squares with sandwich paste and set up Carmen's scraps of cardboard. There we have it, the ugliest chess set in the whole of New York City.

Carmen thinks for an age, then plays pawn g4, just like Seb Giles. That and pawn h4 are pretty much the worst opening moves that White can play.

'Fric,' I say.

Carmen looks up. 'Did you just call me a freak?'

'Not you, the opening,' I say. 'It's Fric's Opening. Sometimes called the Grob. It doesn't get played a lot.'

'Call me a freak again and I'll cut you.'

I clench my jaw and push a central pawn. I should never have said yes to this game, but we've started now and there's no way back.

Carmen puts a bishop on h3. A legal move but totally absurd. 'Your go,' she says.

I push another central pawn.

My opponent bites her lower lip and crinkles her eyes like a drug mule trying to evacuate a packet of smack. She thinks for like ten minutes and then moves her bishop back to its home square. I want to scream and shout and disembowel myself but there's nothing sharp to hand so I keep my cool and play knight f6.

Carmen rests her chin on her hands and plunges into deep thought. At least, I think that's what it is. Perhaps she has died of idiocy.

'Quick game's a good game,' I murmur.

Carmen looks up. 'What did you say?'

'Nothing. You might want to move a bit quicker, that's all.'

'Are you disrespecting me?'

'Course not.' I glance up at her. 'But they can only detain us here for seventy-two hours.'

A peal of laughter from the benches shows that the other women are listening in. For Carmen, that's the final straw.

She grabs the collar of my jacket, hauls me to my feet and slaps me hard across the face.

I stagger backward. The cons gasp a collective 'woah' of disapproval and excitement.

'Seventy-two hours?' Carmen advances on me with a fierce stare. 'You think that's funny, runt?'

She hits me again, but this time I'm ready for it. I flinch away from the blow, dissipating its power. Another gasp from the cons, and a hoarse shout: *Go, girl!*

I stay on my feet and put up my hands to defend my face. Carmen swings at me again, but I block the blow with my forearm and throw a jab of my own which hits Carmen on the tip of her nose. She staggers backward and bellows in anger.

Here she comes yet again, fists flailing, thirsty for blood. I'm shocked and scared and my eyes are watering but I keep my right hand up to shield my face and keep on jabbing with my left hand, just like I do with my punchbag at home. Most of my blows hit thin air but some of them connect with my attacker's cheeks and temples. She gasps and snarls and comes at me again, and right in the middle of my white-hot terror I am LOVING this.

In my bedroom I can jab a heavy punchbag 74 times in 30 seconds and I can keep going for more than five minutes. But Carmen is not a punchbag and there is nothing neat or predictable about this fight. She moves from side to side and hits back hard, sneaking punch after punch past my right-hand guard, making me reel and splutter. I can hardly see her through the veil of water in my eyes but I keep parrying and punching until out of nowhere I feel a massive blow on my jaw that shoots pain down the whole left side of my body. My legs have gone from under me. I'm on the black and white tiled floor and she's on top of me, hitting me as hard as she can.

Stop. Please stop. Am I saying it out loud or just thinking? I don't even know anymore. But stop is exactly what she does, suddenly and unexpectedly, leaving me groaning and bleeding on the chessboard tiles.

NEXT

'You okay, hon?'

A kind voice pierces my pain. For a moment I think it's Mom, but then I open my swollen eyes and remember where I am. Dora is looking down at me, stroking my hair.

'Hello,' I croak.

'Hey,' says Dora. 'You want the good news or the bad news?'

I sit up slowly and painfully. 'Bad.'

'Bad news is you look like you been run over by a monster truck.' Dora smiles. 'Good news is, no more chess with Carmen. The COs have taken her to another holding cell. Oh, and they're fast-tracking your arraignment.'

'What does that mean?'

'It means they feel bad that a white girl got her face smashed in. You'll meet your attorney soon enough, then go before the judge.'

Ten minutes later a CO arrives holding two blue slips of paper. He calls our names, me and Anna, and confirms our dates of birth. Then he leads us along a corridor, up a yellow cinderblock staircase and into another holding cell.

Kit and the kibitzers are already there.

It may just be relief at getting out of that holding cell, but as soon as I see Kit, I feel weirdly happy. Sure, he's cocky and boss-eyed and his poetry shtick can be kind of tiresome. But he's also clever. And generous. And he cares what happens to me, which is more than can be said for most people.

'Leah, your face!' cries Kit. 'What happened?'

'Took one for the team. I figured if someone beat up on me we'd get our arraignment fast-tracked.'

Kit stands there gaping at me, clutching his beltless jeans to stop them falling down. Here's the really shocking thing. He and I have known each other for no time at all and already he's the closest thing I have to a friend in the whole world.

Anna rolls her eyes. 'What the moral moron is trying to say is that she had a chessboxing session with a murderer and lost. It was like watching a bout at the Elephant Club, except a whole lot shorter.'

An officer unlocks the cell door and a man shuffles in. At first I think he's another con, because he is unshaven and looks like he's slept in his clothes. But then I see his clipboard and realize that this is the Public Defender, our attorney. He introduces himself as Mr Butts, which makes the patzers snigger.

'Here's where we're at,' says Mr Butts. 'You were apprehended under Section two hundred and forty, clause thirty-five of the New York Penal Code. Loitering in a public place for the purpose of gambling. You three' – he points at me, Kit and Anna – 'were playing chess and receiving money. You three' – he points at the kibitzers – 'were placing bets on games. You will be arraigned as a group, all six of you together. I've talked to the arresting officers and the Public Prosecutor and they have a strong case. They've got video evidence, and not just the Park Girl video, either. There are closed circuit cameras hidden in trees all around the park.'

'What if we plead ignorance?' says Kit.

'Ignorance of the law is no defense. Besides, there are signs next to the chess tables that specifically prohibit gambling.'

'And the sentence?'

'Five hundred dollar fine and up to ninety days in jail. I've asked for leniency in view of your ages, but the NYPD is pressing for the harshest penalty. They want to make an example of you.'

Anna's face crumples. She puts a hand over her mouth and starts crying. 'I can't go to jail,' she sobs through her fingers. 'I'll lose my student visa.'

'Anna Ivanova and Leah Baxter, you two are also being charged with resisting arrest.' Mr Butts shifts his weight miserably to the other foot. 'There's a chance they might drop that one, but only if you plead guilty to the loitering charge.'

'I'm going to get kicked out of the country,' says Anna. 'Two and a half years of hard work, all for nothing.'

The patzers tut and shake their heads in sympathy.

'Hey, Kit,' I whisper. 'Is chessboxing an actual thing? Anna talked about it like it's a thing.'

'Yes, it's a thing,' he whispers back. 'It's played all over the world. A round of chess followed by a round of boxing and so on and so on until checkmate or knockout. They hold prize bouts at the Elephant Club on Saturday nights.'

'You ever been to watch?'

'No.'

Mr Butts clears his throat loudly. 'You'll be called into court soon,' he says. 'When you go in, don't motion to anyone and don't say a word. Just sit where you're told and look straight ahead. If the judge asks you to confirm your name, do so briefly and then be quiet again. Let me do the talking.'

'You got that, Leah?' says Kit. 'Let Mr Butts do the talking.'

I suddenly feel nervous again, like when we first arrived at Central Booking. 'Sure,' I mutter. 'You won't even know I'm there.'

Ten minutes later we're summoned into the arraignment courtroom. I walk through the reinforced door and sit down in the dock with the other hustlers. At last, a room that doesn't reek of urine.

Through the slits of my swollen eyes, I see police officers, security personnel and earnest young attorneys buzzing around at the front of the room. Up in the public gallery, spectators slouch in wooden pews. And even though I'm about to go to jail for three months, I keep thinking about chessboxing. *A round of chess followed by a round of boxing and so on and so on until checkmate or knockout.*

Just beautiful.

The arraignment judge has cold blue eyes, glasses and gray hair pulled back into a tight bun. She makes us confirm our names and then asks the Public Prosecutor to sum up the case against us.

He springs up from his chair, peers at a sheaf of paper in his hand and starts to read: 'According to the Penal Code of the City of New York, a person is guilty of loitering when he or she remains in a public place for the purpose of gambling with cards, dice or other gambling paraphernalia. A person engages in gambling when he or she stakes something of value upon the outcome of a contest of chance or a future contingent event not under his control or influence, upon an agreement that he will receive something of value in the event of a certain outcome.'

The Public Prosecutor removes his glasses with a flourish. He peers at us as if expecting us to applaud his reading skill and in that moment – *zap!* – a familiar jolt at the back of my mind tells me that my position might not be as bleak as I imagined.

The Public Prosecutor continues to address the court. 'Video evidence from earlier today clearly shows the six defendants staking money on the outcome of games of chess, an activity prohibited by a large sign near the chess tables. It's a straightforward case.'

The judge turns to the Mr Butts. 'What is the defendants' plea?'

'Guilty,' intones Mr Butts.

'Not guilty!' I call.

The hum in the public gallery rises to a hubbub. Mr Butts flinches like he has been slapped. The judge glares at me over her glasses.

'Sorry,' I say. 'We were going to plead guilty, but I just realized something. Chess is excluded by the definition of gambling he just read.'

'How so?'

'It is not a contest of chance.'

The judge turns to the Public Prosecutor, who responds fluently, almost smugly, 'If the defendant were familiar with the Penal Code, Your Honor, she would know that a contest of chance is defined as any contest in which the outcome depends in a material degree upon an element of chance, *notwithstanding that skill may also be a factor therein.*'

All eyes are back on me, so I lick my lips and speak again. 'Skill is more than just a factor, Your Honor. Chess is a game of perfect information. At every moment in the game, both players are perfectly informed of all the events that have previously occurred. There is no element of chance at all.'

'But the signs in the park,' snaps the prosecutor. 'They say no gambling.'

'That's my point. According to the Penal Code we weren't gambling.'

The Public Prosecutor opens his mouth and closes it again. He puts on his glasses and takes them off again. He is rattled and everyone in the arraignment courtroom knows it. 'Your Honor,' he splutters. 'There is precedent. Chess hustlers have been convicted of gambling in New York City since before this young lady was even born.'

'Those convictions are unsafe,' I say. 'If I were you I would see to it that the Penal Code is rewritten to include games of perfect information as well as contests of chance.'

'What about resisting arrest?' sneers the Public Prosecutor. 'Should we rewrite the law on that as well?'

'Of course not,' I say. 'But the arresting officers did not formally identify themselves as police, so we had no way of knowing who they were.'

An audible gasp arises from the public gallery. The Prosecutor waves a hand as if trying to swat away my objection. Kit turns and gazes at me like I'm Mikhail Tal or Wonder Woman or better.

The judge turns to address the arresting officers. 'Is that true?' she asks. 'Did you neglect to formally identify yourselves as police officers before chasing these young people through the park?'

An officer half rises. 'We were in uniform, Your Honor.'

'So what?' I retort. 'There was a pillow fight in that park today. Almost everybody was wearing some kind of crazy-ass costume.'

A gale of laughter rises from the wooden pews in the public gallery.

'Silence!' The judge glares up at the gallery and then down at me. 'Young lady, hold your tongue. Interrupt the proceedings of this arraignment once more and I will hold you in contempt.'

I sneak a sideways glance at Kit. His shoulders are shaking and he's holding his nose, trying to stop himself laughing.

'I am disinclined to continue with this charade,' continues the judge. 'Regardless of what costumes were in evidence in Washington Square Park today, a person can only be convicted of resisting arrest if the arresting officers formally identify themselves as NYPD. As for the loitering charge, I play a little chess myself and I grant that chess is indeed a game of perfect information containing no material element of chance. Rather than waste time and money bringing this hopeless case to trial, I hereby dismiss the charges against all six defendants. I will recommend to the City of New York that the perfect information loophole be closed as soon as possible. As for you, Miss Baxter' – she fixes me with a gimlet eye – 'you are arrogant, impertinent and unbearably cocksure. I recommend a career in law.'

'Thank you, Your Honor.'

'Court dismissed. You are free to go.'

BREAKROOM

We wait by a potted palm in the courtroom lobby while a court official stalks off to reclaim our bags, belts, shoelaces and phones. Kit and the kibitzers are flushed with victory, high-fiving and chest-bumping like varsity basketball players. Mr Butts, however, is sullen and sarcastic. He has taken a dislike to me because I did his job for him and made him look like a douche. Anna sits apart with her face in her hands, relieved to the point of tears, her American dream unexpectedly risen from the Tombs. As for me, my cheeks and jaw are aching like crazy and my eyes are so swollen I can hardly see.

As soon as we get our phones back, we go straight online. The chess arrests are all over Twitter. One of many photos doing the rounds shows me vaulting over the stone chess bench to get away from the Feds. Another shows Anna face down on the grass being cuffed. People are calling us the Washington Square Six. Some of their tweets link back to the Park Girl video.

'Wait until the news gets out about your performance at the arraignment,' laughs Kit. 'It'll break the internet.'

'It's not the internet you should be worrying about,' says Mr Butts morosely. 'It's the regular press. I guarantee you that five minutes from now the sidewalk outside Central Booking will be heaving with reporters and photographers wanting a piece of you. You should get outta here before they arrive.'

'Good idea.' Kit grasps Mr Butts warmly by the hand. 'Thank you for representing us, sir. It's true, you only said one word at our arraignment, and it's true the word was "Guilty", but you said it loud and clear and with just the right amount of gravitas. Never compound ignorance with inaudibility, that's what I always say.'

Leaving the Public Defender scowling darkly next to the potted palm, we head for the door and barge out into the warm April evening.

'Freedom!' shouts Kit, dancing a jig on the marble steps. 'Let's go play chess!'

'No,' I say. 'What I need right now is a burger the size of my head.'

Anna and the kibitzers are heading straight home. We say goodbye to them and go our separate ways.

Kit takes me to a burger joint called Breakroom, a tiny joint squashed in between a bail bond office and an acupuncturist.

It has shared tables, dim lights and bare brick walls. I order the house burger with fries, onion rings and a pitcher of pomegranate lemonade. Kit orders a chili cheese jalapeno dog. My saliva glands are going crazy already.

'Tell me something, Leah,' says Kit. 'Did you trip Anna on purpose?'

'Of course I did.'

Kit laughs and shakes his head. He reaches into his bag and takes out a book. 'I think this is yours,' he says. 'You left it on the chess table this morning when you made your sudden departure.'

'Reshevsky!' I grab the book. 'Thank you! I thought I'd never see it again.'

Kit tosses his head in mock annoyance. 'When someone gives you a gift, you should take better care of it.'

The pitcher of lemonade arrives. I scoop out a handful of ice and hold it to my aching face.

'This is nice,' says Kit. 'Central Booking wouldn't make any TripAdvisor Top Ten lists, but it was totally worth it to get a date with you.'

'This isn't a date.' I lean across the table to shove a chunk of ice down the neck hole of his T-shirt. He grabs the ice, squirming and shrieking, wrestling it away from its target.

'House burger and jalapeno dog,' says the server, plonking our food on the table.

We come apart and sober up. 'Sorry,' Kit mutters. 'My date was being mean.'

The server shrugs and goes away. Steam rises off the spicy beef, fried egg and onion rings. I feel happy.

'I want you to come with me to the Elephant Club tonight,' I say. 'I don't want to wait another week before going.'

Kit looks at me with a half-smile. He takes a bite of his jalapeno dog and chews it slowly before responding.

'Chessboxing is dumb,' he says at last.

'How do you know? You've never even watched it.'

'The concept is dumb. It's just nerds fighting.'

'No it's not,' I say, talking with my mouth full. 'It sounds like the most perfect battle you can imagine between two human beings. The ultimate contest of brains and brawn. Anyways, you're coming with me whether you like it or not, because if it weren't for me, you wouldn't be eating that jalapeno dog right now. You'd be in jail eating gross-out sandwiches and carving the first of ninety strikes into the wall.'

'If it weren't for *you*, we wouldn't have been arrested in the first place. I told you not to play Roderick Wilde and you ignored me.'

'Shush.' I shove a forkful of fries into his mouth. 'You're coming with me to the Elephant Club to watch the chessboxing. Deal with it.'

Kit chews the fries ruefully, then lifts his head to the high ceiling and shrieks at the top of his voice: 'LA BELLE DAME SANS MERCI HATH ME IN THRALL!'

The server drops a pile of plates and kicks us out for causing a disturbance.

TWENTY-FIVE THINGS ABOUT KIT

We take the subway to Hell's Kitchen, then walk and talk all the way to the club. On the way, I learn a whole bunch of stuff about Kit.

1. He is sixteen years old.

2. He has a huge family: mother, father, three brothers and two sisters.

3. They rent an apartment above a Ramen noodle bar in West Harlem.

4. They have to keep their windows closed even in summertime, because of the overpowering smell of picante beef noodle broth.

5. Kit's grandparents were all Irish.

6. His parents moved to America in 1995, before he was born.

7. His grandfather Seamus McTarnsay was a famous poet back in Ireland.

8. The McTarnsays have always been poets.

9. They have always been chess players too. Seamus McTarnsay played correspondence chess with people all over the world. Cost him a fortune in postage stamps.

10. Kit's parents both play. They taught Kit when he was three years old, using the website chessat3.com.

11. He has never seen *Star Wars*.

12. He has never seen a Superbowl final.

13. He has never seen an episode of *America's Got Talent*.

14. When he is not playing chess, he memorizes poetry for pleasure.

15. He doesn't know how many poems he has memorized.

16. His current favorite is a Coleridge poem called 'Dejection'.

17. He goes to Park East High School.

18. During vacations Kit used to run a 'Poetry for Peanuts' stall in Washington Square Park.

19. Love-addled customers would pay him to write love poetry for significant others.

20. When Kit saw Nathan Banks playing chess in the park, he realized there was more money in chess hustling than in love poetry.

21. They formed the Poisoned Pawns two years ago.

22. They only play during vacations.

23. Kit McTarnsay is an anagram of ARTY STICKMAN.

24. His full name Christopher McTarnsay is an anagram of STERN MATRIARCH PSYCHO.

25. Kit's dream is to travel the world, playing chess and writing poetry. Clearly a romantic.

ELEPHANT CLUB

A long line of people snakes along the sidewalk from the door of the Elephant Club all the way back to the Rent-a-Car building at the end of the block. They are joshing and taking selfies, giddy with anticipation.

Kit and I join the line and shuffle slowly forward past a huge billboard advertising tonight's chessboxing event. The schedule has six live bouts, including a championship bout between Zach 'The Destroyer' Baker and Igor 'The Eyes' Ivanovitch. There's a women's bout too. Sydney 'Shock and Awe' Campbell versus Padmini 'The Mosquito' Khan.

I can't wait to see this strange hybrid sport. Blood is pumping in my ears and I've got this dizzy feeling, like somehow I am brushing against my destiny.

When we finally reach the door, two bouncers bar our way, biceps bulging beneath their tailored shirts.

When they see my face they can't help staring. 'This one looks like she's been in a few rounds with Sydney Campbell already,' jokes one.

'Sorry, sweetheart,' says the other, 'but this is a nightclub. You need to be twenty-one to come in.'

'I *am* twenty-one.'

'What about you?' He turns to Kit.

'Twenty-one,' says Kit, and then like an idiot he embellishes the lie. 'We both turned twenty-one yesterday.'

'Yesterday? Both of you?'

'We're twins. This is our birthday treat.'

'You don't look like twins.'

'I know.' Kit's face is turning puce. 'I don't mean we're twinned with each other. I mean we're twinned with other people. Different people.'

'You got age ID?'

'No.'

'Hop it, both of you.'

'Sure.'

We're so good at getting thrown out of places they should give us medals for it. We walk back up the street in silence until I can no longer contain my frustration.

'Birthday treat? Are you for real?'

Kit raises his hands in a Don't Shoot kind of way. 'I'm sorry, I'm no good at lying. And anyways, that guy wasn't going to believe us, whatever we said.'

'We're twins, but not with each other? What the actual—?'

'I said I'm sorry, all right? Let's go someplace and get a milkshake. My treat.'

'No, let's check around the back of the club. See if there's another way in.'

Kit knows that arguing with me is as pointless as arguing with the bouncers on the door. He follows me around the back of the block and along a dark alley full of fire escapes and air-conditioning units. There is a fire door which might belong to the club, but there's no handle on the door and no other way of getting in.

My heart is heavy as we traipse back up the alley toward the Rent-a-Car building. I had an appointment with destiny and destiny stood me up just like she always does.

'Milkshake?' says Kit.

'I guess.'

Scaffold has been erected up the side of the Rent-a-Car building. It covers three floors, all the way up to the roof. Out of nowhere a mate-in-three jolt flashes across my brain. I open the map app on my phone and switch to satellite view.

'What now?' Kit cranes his neck to look. 'We don't need a map, Leah. I know a place on Forty-Second Street where we can get a cookie dough milkshake as big as the World Junior Chess Trophy. I can find it blindfold.'

I zoom in on the Elephant Club and tilt the screen toward Kit. 'Shut up and look at this. The Elephant Club has a roof bar.'

'So what?'

'So that's our way in. All we have to do is climb the scaffold, run along the roofs to the bar and go on down into the club.'

'You're kidding. The ladders are in full view of the traffic intersection. We'd have a hundred people calling nine-one-one before we got ten feet off the ground. Besides, I thought you were scared of heights.'

'I am. So if I can do it, you definitely can. Come on, Kit, I really want to see this.'

Kit shakes his head and starts walking off. I chase after him and pester him like you wouldn't believe, but he's adamant.

135

No, he's not going to climb the scaffold. No, he's not going to run along the roof. And no, he's still not interested in chessboxing. Not even if we call the whole thing a date.

'I don't get you, Leah,' Kit says. 'It's like you're on this dumb adrenalin trip that gets more dangerous and messed up by the minute. Hustling and prison not enough for you now? You need some bloodletting with your board games?'

'Just living my life,' I snap back. 'Carping the diem. Gathering rosebuds while I may. You're the poet, you should know that stuff.'

He folds his arms and looks at me, tender and wonky-eyed. 'Your dad isn't in space, is he, Leah?'

Pow. The unexpected attack comes out of nowhere and I've got nothing, no defense at all.

'Who says he isn't?'

'The NASA website,' he says. 'There's only one American at the International Space Station right now, and she's a woman.'

'My dad's on his way back.'

Silence.

'You need to talk about it,' says Kit softly. '*The grief that does not speak whispers the o'er-fraught heart and bids it break.*'

'You quoting Hamlet at me?' I advance toward him and grab him by the throat. 'Tell me you didn't just quote Hamlet at me.'

'Macbeth,' croaks Kit.

I push him away from me hard, then turn around and walk. I can imagine the shock and hurt on his face, same as when I socked him outside that tattoo parlor, but I honestly don't care. He is calling me back but I ignore him and carry on walking toward the Rent-a-Car building. My mouth is dry, my palms are sweating and I'm shaking like a smackhead in the Tombs. I need to get inside that club right now. I need a noisy crowd in which to lose myself.

VERTIGO

Kit was right about the ladders being visible from the intersection. I figure the safest route is to stay away from the ladders and shin up the inside of the frame between the poles and the wall. But first I need to find a way over the hoarding which protects the base of the scaffold.

A large dumpster next to the hoarding provides my way in. I climb on top of it, haul myself up the hoarding and slither down the other side. Signs hanging from the first tier of scaffold scream their warnings at me. STRICTLY NO ENTRY reads one. TRESPASSERS WILL BE PROSECUTED threatens another. The thought of finding myself back in the Tombs for the night makes me feel sick, but I'm the wrong side of the hoarding now and there's no way back to the street.

I press my back to the wall, grip the cold iron scaffold with both hands and start to hoist myself up through the eighteen-inch gap between wall and scaffold. I move quickly, muscling up two feet at a time, using the friction of the rough brickwork to hold me steady as I reposition my hands. *Don't look down. Don't look down. Don't look down.*

Between the first and second floors of the building, my path is blocked by a concrete ledge sticking out from the wall, so I swivel my body around to the other side of the pole and continue to hoist myself up. Progress is harder now with nothing to press back against. *Stay strong*, I tell myself. My biceps are burning and my hands are slick with sweat, but somehow I maneuver past the concrete ledge. I heave myself onto a crossbrace to catch my breath, and that's when I see it, mounted on the scaffold frame a few feet above me.

A scaffold alarm.

I have no idea what sort of alarm it is. Perhaps it is triggered by vibrations in the scaffold frame, or maybe infrared motion detectors. I should have guessed the scaffold would be rigged with alarms. Who leaves thousands of dollars' worth of metal hanging around unprotected in the middle of Hell's Kitchen? Mr Freaking Nobody, that's who.

Kit was right. This climb was a terrible idea.

Perched on the cross-brace with my feet dangling in thin air, panic rises in my chest. *Go back down*, I tell myself. *Only a total douchebag gets arrested twice in one day.* I shuffle forward off the bar and let my arms take my weight.

I'm all set to slide back down, but I don't. Instead I find myself climbing up toward the alarm with a brain full of noise like a juggernaut crunching gears.

Blow the farm on the Powerball
Molotov Me will sabotage it all!

Back to the wall, hands on the scaffold, I haul myself up two feet at a time. To my left, bolted to the scaffold frame, a motion sensor winks at me. I stare back at it. A high-pitched siren sounds from the alarm box.

This pleasure dome is doomed to fall
Molotov Me will sabotage it all!

The ear-splitting blare of the intruder alarm gives strength to my tired muscles. I power on upward past the second and third floors and haul myself onto the roof.

Fly high, Molotov Me!
Sky high, Molotov Me!

I roll off the parapet onto the rooftop, a solid surface at last. Spread out before me are pipes, vents, air-conditioning units and access hatches. Down below me the alarm continues to screech.

An access hatch opens and two men in security uniforms emerge onto the roof. I crawl behind a large A/C unit, and crouch there, muscles tense, as the men pick their way across the roof toward me. They have flashlights in their hands and guns in their belts.

I'm out of options. I stand up, raise my hands above my head and step out into the crisscrossing flashlight beams. At least, that's what a normal person would do. What I actually do (because I'm a moral moron) is to pull up the hood of my jacket, roll into the shadow of a thick metal pipe and start wriggling across the roof on my stomach. Out of the corner of my eye I see the security men peering over the parapet, shining their flashlights across the scaffold below.

Fly high, Molotov Me!
Sky high, Molotov Me!

In the right position, with a clear route to promotion, a pawn can beat two knights. If he can reach the far end of the board without being captured, that humble pawn transforms into a knight, a bishop, a rook or (most commonly) a queen.

Heart pounding, I wriggle over a low concrete wall onto the next roof and dart across it in a low crouch, vaulting over vents and hatches as I go.

'Hey, you! Stop!'

I glance back. A flashlight shines in my eyes. They've spotted me.

I stand up and run full speed toward a high brick wall which I'm guessing is the back wall of the Elephant Club roof bar.

It's much too high to vault, this wall, so I'll have to go around it. I sprint to the edge of the building, hop onto the parapet and press my hands against the bricks, digging my fingertips into the shallow mortar ruts. I can hear people talking and laughing on the other side, enjoying a drink before the show begins.

'Stop right there! Freeze!'

I ignore the guard's commands and begin to teeter around the edge of the wall, the parapet beneath my feet tapering off into a narrow ledge no more than two inches wide. I'm on tiptoes, pressing my whole body against the bricks, shuffling sideways in tiny increments. I hardly dare breathe, let alone look down. One gust of wind could send me tumbling into the abyss.

My heart speeds up until it feels like it is going to ram right through my chest. My ribs and lungs feel tight.

Then come the thoughts:

I'm going to slip. I'm going to fall. I'm going to fall and die. I should have gone with Kit. I should have gone for that milkshake. I should be at home wrapped up in my crocodile onesie. I should have played d5 in Pune and let Sivenko exchange knights. I should have stayed with Dad instead of going to Rhode Island.

'Stay where you are, ma'am.' The tone of the guards has changed. 'Just hold on. We're coming to get you!'

I imagine coming down off my aching tiptoes, slipping gracefully off the ledge and falling through the cool night air.

I'm not going to fall but I am going to throw up.

I'm not going to throw up, but I am going to fall.

I'm not going to fall. I am going to get a grip.

I imagine forcing the panic down into my belly, and locking it there with a silver key. I imagine staying on my tiptoes and shuffling six more painful inches to my left.

Remember Reshevsky, I tell myself. *My strength consists of a fighting spirit, a great desire to win, and a stubborn defense whenever in trouble.*

The roof bar of the Elephant Club is bordered by a chest-high metal railing. I imagine extending my left arm toward that rail. I imagine grabbing it firmly. I imagine pulling myself across and vaulting the rail to safety.

I imagine, therefore I do.

I'm in a dim-lit corner of the bar with favela funk pounding in my ears. Two airheads with their backs to me are in the middle of taking a selfie. They zoom in on the photo, do a cartoonish double-take and whirl around to stare at me. They are wearing identical crop tops, holding identical cocktails and gawping with identical frowns of confusion.

'Where did you spring from?' says one.

'You appeared out of like *nowhere*,' says the other.

I grab a glass of root beer off a nearby table. 'Don't know what you mean,' I say, pushing through the crowd toward the stairs.

FIGHT CLUB

I slide down two sets of banisters and push through a heavy fire door into a seething mass of guys and girls. They stand shoulder to shoulder, laughing, arguing, dancing and yelling idiotic nothings into each other's earholes. This is the mezzanine floor of the club, a dingy horseshoe-shaped gallery which overlooks a bright-lit boxing ring. Inside the ring a chess table and two chairs have been set up.

My phone pings. It's a message from Kit.

Leah, I'm here for you any time you want to talk.

I switch off my phone and shove it in my pocket. Talking is overrated.

In front of the chess table a woman dressed in a sequined spacesuit is singing 'Fly Me to the Moon'. To the left of the ring a dozen officials hunch over laptops. Hovering behind them stands a grizzled grandmaster who I recognize as Marcus Crockett, one of the strongest chess players in New York. I played him at the Brooklyn Open when I was thirteen, and ended up beating him in a fiendish bishop endgame. Still have the newspaper clippings to prove it.

I push my way to the back of the hall and down a metal staircase onto the ground floor.

'Hey,' says a husky voice.

I turn around and see the guy from the park, the one who offered to be my bodyguard. He is wearing a silver necklace and a too-tight T-shirt.

'Oh,' I say. 'Hello, jock.'

'Travis,' he says. He is staring with concern at the bruises on my face. 'What happened to you?'

'I'm fine.'

'I told you chess hustlers are a magnet for trouble. Didn't I tell you that?'

'Yes, you told me. Congratulations. And no, I still don't want a bodyguard.'

Spacewoman finishes her song, flings her arms wide and leaps into the crowd. A cacophony of cheers breaks out as the singer crowd-surfs back and forth over our heads.

'You don't look twenty-one,' says Travis. 'How did you get in here?'

'Climbed the scaffold around the back. You?'

'I know everyone here. This is my sport.'

'Really?' I look at him properly for the first time. 'You're a chessboxer?'

Travis nods. 'July tenth, it'll be me in that ring. My fifth bout.'

'How did the first four go?'

'I won two of them by KO. I'm the best middleweight boxer on the circuit. Everyone says so.'

Most arrogant too, by the sound of it. 'What about the other two bouts?' I ask.

'I would have won on points, but my chess let me down.' He looks away. 'That's why I wanted your help.'

A second spotlight flicks on, illuminating a metal DJ booth suspended above us. More favela funk blasts out across the crowd. Strobe lights flow across upturned faces. The crowd buzzes with feverish anticipation.

'Ladies and gentlemen,' a voice booms over the PA system. 'Please welcome your host, *Marcus Crockett*!'

The spectators surge forward to get even closer to the boxing ring. I surge too, pushing my way through to the front. Travis follows.

Marcus Crockett bounds into the ring shouting, 'Yeah!' and 'Bring it!' and other horsefeathers. He introduces the boxing referee, a wiry dude whose bald head glistens under the spotlights.

Crockett introduces the women's middleweight bout. He invites the crowd to welcome Sydney 'Shock and Awe' Campbell. The crowd scream and clap.

The opening bars of *Lose Yourself* blare from the booth above our heads. A magnificent gowned figure strides down the central aisle, leaps into the red corner and throws back her hood. She has black skin, high cheekbones, short twists of braided hair and a scowl that could drop an ox.

'Army girl,' Travis shouts in my ear. 'Enlisted when she was seventeen. Served in Iraq and Afghanistan. Won the US Armed Forces Chess Open three times running. And now she does this. We train in the same gym.'

Facing Sydney Campbell tonight is an Indian chessboxer Padmini 'The Mosquito' Khan. Bollywood music blares from the amps as the Mosquito dances down the aisle and into the ring.

I ask Travis why they call her the Mosquito and he grins. 'It's because she's so hard to swat. One of the most mobile fighters I've ever seen. The other women can't get near her, and that makes them mad, which in turn makes them vulnerable. And before they know it, she's right up close, drinking their blood.'

'What about her chess?'

'Brutal. You wouldn't think it to look at her, but she's one of the most aggressive chess players on the circuit.'

Padmini Khan bounces around the ring on the balls of her feet, then sits down at the chessboard opposite Sydney Campbell. They put on headphones to drown out the commentary, and Marcus Crockett starts the clocks. They're off.

CAMPBELL VERSUS KHAN

The women play the opening quickly and confidently, their bandaged hands the only hint of the violence to come. e4. e5. Nf3. Nc6. Bb5. The American girl plays a Marshall Attack. The Indian defends solidly. Two huge screens on either side of the hall relay the game to the crowd, and

Marcus Crockett commentates for the sake of the newbs and patzers. Both women are playing suboptimal moves all over the place, but after four minutes the position is roughly even.

'Round two,' shouts Travis in my ear. 'Boxing.'

Deft stagehands whisk the chessboard, table and chairs out of the ring. A card girl prances around shaking her booty and the contestants don boxing gloves over their bandaged hands. I am surprised to see they are not wearing protective headgear.

The referee signals for the boxers to engage. As soon as the bell rings, Sydney Campbell lets rip with a flurry of jabs and crosses. Not a single blow connects with Khan, who bobs and weaves around her opponent, luring the American to make wilder and wilder swings.

'Good footwork,' murmurs Travis.

The American winds up her right arm and delivers a haymaker that misses Khan's head by a whisker. The Indian takes her chance and responds with a fierce uppercut of her own. *Bam!*

The skin ripples across Campbell's cheek. She staggers sideways. The bell rings for the chess round.

'Focus, Syd!' yells Travis above the baying crowd.

The table, chairs and chessboard reappear. The fighters sit down, chests heaving.

'Hardest moment for any chessboxer,' says Travis in my ear. 'Sitting down to consider your next move when you've just been hit in the head.'

Sydney Campbell scowls down at the board and pushes her e pawn. Khan castles. Campbell reaches for her queen, then pulls back her hand and thinks again. Her king's pawn is overextended and her confidence is slipping.

'I could do this,' I shout in Travis's ear.

'Really?' He looks at me. 'You boxed before?'

'I've got a punchbag in my room,' I say. 'I can hit it really hard.'

He frowns. 'There's a bit more to it than that.'

Round 4. More boxing. Once again, Khan flits around just out of Campbell's range, then slips inside and hammers her opponent with two jabs and a right cross. The crowd roars.

Travis cups his hands around his mouth. 'Too static, Syd!' he yells. 'Make some angles!'

Another uppercut from the Mosquito sends the American sprawling on the canvas. She gets up on the count of four, but her eyes are groggy, unfocussed.

'Too old, too slow,' I say. 'If she were ten years younger, she would splat that mosquito in five seconds flat.'

'If she were your age, you mean?'

'Sure.'

The bell rings. The chessboard reappears. Campbell slumps in her seat and shakes her head, struggling to focus on the pieces in front of her.

Travis glances at me sideways. 'Do you dance?' he says.

'No. Why?'

'Khan was a Kathak dancer before she was ever a boxer. That's why her footwork is so good. I just figured, if you like dancing . . .'

'I don't.'

I turn back to the chess. The American is lost in a mental fog and her next move is a blunder. Marcus Crockett sucks in air through his teeth and starts to gabble excitedly. Khan moves quickly, sensing that the win is near. But before she can deliver the killer blow, the bell rings.

'The next boxing round will be brutal,' says Travis. 'Sydney knows she is about to get mated on the board, so she needs a knockout in the next three minutes. She'll come out of her corner like a woman possessed.'

Possessed is right. As soon as the bell rings, Campbell shoots out of her corner and charges toward her opponent like a Pamplona bull. She shrugs off two jabs from the Mosquito and catches her with a beautiful left hook of her own. As the

Indian staggers backward, Campbell steps inside and delivers a crunching body punch.

A barbaric roar rises from the crowd. Khan is on the ropes, gloves up to her face, ducking and dodging and trying to pivot away to one side, but that body punch has slowed her down and Campbell is on her with a six-punch combo so brutal it makes me wince.

Khan's hair is loose. She is bleeding from her nose. Her left eye is closing up. She hits the ropes and bounces back into another hard left hook.

'You got her, Syd!' yells Travis, as the Mosquito of Uttar Pradesh hits the floor.

On the count of seven Khan drags herself to her feet, but she is no longer flitting gracefully as before. Her wings are clipped. Her spirit is gone. She is hurt and scared and playing for time.

'Finish her, Sydney!' I hear myself yell.

Cameras flash. Music pounds. The crowd presses around me, primal, euphoric. I long more than anything to be inside that ring, dancing and punching and being punched.

With thirty seconds to go, the women square up to each other and fight inside each other's guard, matching each other blow for blow, slugging it out in a desperate bid to be the last woman standing. Sydney Campbell crouches low to duck a wild left hook, then up she comes with a perfect uppercut to Khan's jaw.

The Mosquito hits the canvas and does not get up.

Marcus Crockett grabs the soldier's hand and thrusts it high above her head. Her pummeled face lights up in a beatific smile.

I'm cheering and stamping with the crowd and I've got the exact same feeling I had thirteen years ago when I first found a plastic chess set in the games cupboard at home and opened it up to examine the pieces.

I've played chess since I was four. I've shadow boxed since I was seven. Dad and I both knew I was going to be World Champion one day and of course we both assumed it would be for classical chess. Maybe we were wrong.

Chessboxing champion of the world. That would make Dad proud for sure. Destiny is knocking on my door so hard her fist is splintering the panels.

I turn to Travis and yell above the noise of the crowd, 'Where do you train?'

'Bert's Gym,' he says. 'I'll take you there tomorrow, if you like.'

It's gone midnight when I get back home but Mom has stayed up waiting for me. As soon as she hears my footsteps in the corridor she flies out to meet me in a What Time Do You Call This rage.

Then she sees the bruises on my face.

'Leah! What happened? Are you all right?'

I was expecting this reaction and I have already practiced my story. I tell Mom it was an accident. I was carrying a tray of donuts out of the bake room at Gonuts Donuts this afternoon and the swing door flew back and hit me in the face.

'Come,' she says, hurrying into the kitchen. 'You need ice. Lots and lots of ice.'

Two minutes later, I'm lying on my bed and Mom is pressing two huge bags of frozen peas against my bruises, calling me her 'poor munchkin' and other excruciating names.

'Tell me what happened,' she murmurs. 'And don't give me that swing door story again. I know that's horsefeathers.'

'What? How?'

'I rang the donut shop before you got back. They said you quit your job yesterday.'

Typical of Mom to call my boss just because I'm a few minutes late arriving home. I have no choice now but to come clean and tell her the truth. She scowls while I explain about quitting my job to play chess in the park, she gawks when I tell her about my arrest and incarceration, and when I describe getting beaten up by Carmen the psychopath she drops her jaw like a study for one of those bug-eyed Munch paintings. After that I figure I have nothing to lose, so I double down and tell her I've decided to become a chessboxer.

'Chessboxing is perfect for me,' I say. 'I start my training tomorrow.'

'No, you don't,' Mom snaps. 'You're grounded.'

'For how long?'

'Forever.'

Mom presses the frozen peas against my face and she's not calling me munchkin anymore, she's ranting about how ashamed she is of my behavior and how I've gone off the rails since Dad died and how I make her life harder and harder with every day that passes. As she talks on and on, she squeezes the freezer bag so hard that it suddenly splits along a seam, showering me with ice-cold peas.

On another day, in another place, in another life, the peas thing might have been hilarious. *Hallelujah, it's raining peas! Look, you're covered in them! Fetch the camera, quick! Everybody say 'PEAS'!*

But this is us, tonight, and I'm not laughing, I'm crying, and before the peas have even stopped bouncing I leap to my feet and round on my mother.

'Okay, you're right, I have gone off the rails. Going off the rails was the best thing I ever did! Can't you see how dumb your rails were? Don't you understand what you did to me? Home-schooled from the age of four. Five hours of chess a day. Coaching. Hotels. Planes. Pressure. Always feeling like I was disappointing you. Your rails were messed up! Dad knew it, but he's not with us anymore.'

Mom's cheeks quiver with anger. 'Don't put that on me, Leah. Your father and I took those decisions together. We saw how much you loved chess, and we did everything we could to help you go as far as you wanted.'

'As far as *you* wanted.'

'That's not true!' Mom grabs my wrist and leads me roughly into her bedroom. She reaches for the memory box at the back of the closet and yanks it out so hard its contents spill across the carpet. 'Look at this,' she says, picking up a child's pencil case. 'I HEART CHESS. I didn't write that, Leah. You did.'

'It happens,' I mutter. 'People fall in love with their kidnappers. It's called Stockholm Syndrome.'

'What about this?' She picks up a grainy polaroid photo, a girl with wonky bangs sitting in front of a massive chessboard.

'That's you at the World Junior Chess Championship. Seven years old. Look at that smile, Leah! Is that the smile of a hostage?'

'Kids smile,' I answer wearily. 'It's what kids do. They smile in refugee camps and they smile in orphanages and they even smile at the World Junior Che—'

'You begged us to enter you in that tournament, Leah. *You begged us.* Not the other way around. But it was in Europe, so I said no way. Too far and too expensive. You begged and cried and eventually your father gave in and booked two flights to Naples, one for you and one for him. Took the week off work and almost lost his job at the university for it. He was so excited for the trip, Leah. Talked about it like it was going to be this epic father-daughter adventure.'

'Stop it, Mom.' We're both ugly-crying now.

'He was right, it was epic. Your first international tournament and you took it by storm. Won the Under-ten category by a country mile. Viktor Nureyev watched your final game, and he told your dad—'

'I know, all right? I was there. He told Dad he'd never seen a child with such a natural flair for the game. Whoopie-doo!'

'That's not all he said, Leah. He also told your father to see to it that you got a proper chess coach.'

'Nureyev said that? I don't remember him saying that.'

'Well, he did. Your father was all of a twitter when I met you both at the airport. Excited, sure, but worried too. He was sure we could never afford a coach.'

'I don't remember that.'

'He loved you being good at chess, Leah. He was so proud of what you did in Naples, he saved up every last dime for tuition and tournaments.'

I look down at the pile of chess stuff from my past and it feels like there's something stuck in my lungs, making it difficult to breathe. 'What are you trying to say, Mom? That I let him down when I quit tournament chess?'

'No.'

'That I've insulted his memory?'

'Of course not.' Mom glares at me through a veil of tears. 'We wanted you to fulfil your potential, that's all.'

'And what if my potential is in hustling or chessboxing?'

Mom's jaw clenches. 'Then I'm saving you a world of hurt by grounding you. I'm serious, Leah. It's for your own good. You will not leave this house until further notice.'

In chess the safety of your king is paramount. He must be protected at all costs. Barricade him in the corner of the board, guard him with a big fat rook, shield him with gallant pawns. Even the most birdbrained of patzers castle early in the game, and if they don't, they soon come to regret it.

Be careful, though. The precious king needs air to breathe. If his protectors press too close, the monarch starts to suffocate and a single knight check is enough to kill him off.

Smothered mate, that's what it's called. In the right position you can force it from four moves out, usually with a double check and a queen sac. Shove your opponent's own rook down his throat and make him choke on it. A dazzling, elegant way to win. A tragicomic way to lose.

Imagine being smothered by your own pieces, condemned to death by your own protectors. The stuff of nightmares, right? Don't worry, it has never happened to me in a tournament and never will. I can spot a smothered mate at a hundred paces, thank you very much.

But, of course, there are more ways to get smothered than over a chessboard. Rook, pawn, mother, coach, so many dumb ways to asphyxiate and die.

I call Travis and tell him I can't come to the gym because I'm grounded. Kind of like Rapunzel, except for my short hair, my high IQ and my apartment being on the first floor.

'How long are you grounded for?' asks Travis.

'Forever, Mom says.'

'Bummer.' A short silence, and then, 'You've got a punchbag in your room, right? Why don't I give you boxing lessons via Skype? How to stand, how to punch, that sort of thing. And when your mom calms down and lets you out, you can come to the gym and we'll fix you up with a sparring partner.'

'Sounds good.' I lie back on my bed. 'What do you want in return?'

'I want you to get me to nineteen hundred at chess.'

'You said eighteen hundred before.'

'I'm ambitious.'

I think about it for a couple of seconds but it's pretty much a no-brainer. I help him with his chess. He helps me with my boxing. We both become kickass chessboxers.

'Okay, jock,' I tell him. 'You got yourself a deal.'

We talk some more and I ask him a bunch of questions to satisfy myself that he's not a psychopath.

It turns out that talking about Travis is something Travis really enjoys doing. It also turns out that he's no more of a psychopath than I am.

Hardly reassuring.

TWENTY-FIVE THINGS ABOUT TRAVIS

1. He is seventeen years old.

2. He lives in a fourth-floor apartment block in Hell's Kitchen.

3. He goes to Beacon High School.

4. He calls his parents by their first names Denise and Reggie instead of Mom and Dad.

5. His sister Brianna is a cheerleader for the Knicks.

6. He has been playing chess since he was eleven and boxing since he was fourteen.

7. His boxing record is thirteen wins to four losses.

8. All four losses came right at the beginning of his fighting career.

9. When he moved up to senior boxing last year, he couldn't get any fights. Adults didn't want to risk their careers by

losing to a teenager, and boys his own age didn't want to step in the ring with him because they were scared of his left hook.

10. He has an amazing left hook. Everyone says so.

11. He is a boy in a man's world. Everyone says so.

12. Getting hit motivates him. When he takes a punch, he hits back with twenty.

13. Someone at school told him about chessboxing.

14. He has been doing it for six months now.

15. It is only a matter of time until he becomes US middleweight chessboxing champion.

16. He has a super-rare competitor's pass that gets him into the Elephant Club.

17. He likes reading.

18. He struggles to recall anything he's read recently.

19. He has forgotten the title of the Bobby Fischer book I recommended to him.

20. He gets up at 5 a.m. every day and runs for an hour.

21. Then he does 100 push-ups, 100 sit-ups, 50 pull-ups, and 30 bar dips.

22. If he suffers now, he can live the rest of his life as a champion.

23. In sixth grade he injured his kneecap playing football. The kneecap went all the way around to the side of his leg. He didn't even cry.

24. In ninth grade he ruptured his left eardrum in a junior title fight. He didn't cry, and went on to win the fight on points. Now he is deaf in his left ear.

25. He's going to Skype me tomorrow night and give me my first boxing lesson.

IF FREEDOM FAIL

When I hang up, there's a message from Kit waiting for me.

Sorry I quoted Macbeth at you

So I reply, **Sorry I got mad at you**

and he replies, **Come to the park for a game of chess**

and I reply, **I can't, I'm grounded**

and he replies, **For what avail the plow or sail, or land or life, if freedom fail?**

and I reply, **I know, it sucks**

I wedge my phone in between *An Opening Repertoire for Black* and *My 60 Memorable Games*, which Mom put back on my bookshelf along with all my other chess books. I adjust my Bluetooth headset and angle the front camera toward the punchbag, wrinkling my nose at the smell of gasoline that lingers on the books.

Skype rings and Travis appears on the screen of my phone. He is wearing a blue boxing vest and his shoulders are pumped and shiny like he's already been working out.

'Hey.' His voice is loud in my earbuds. 'Are you ready to rumble?'

'Sure.'

'Let's get going, then. Put on your gloves and go stand in front of the bag. Don't punch it yet, just stand there with your left shoulder forward and your hands up to your face. That's it. Now put your chin down a little. Bend your knees. Look at the bag over the top of your gloves. Good. Now show me your jab.'

I shield my face with my right hand and drive my left hand into the bag. *Thud.*

'You need to loosen up,' says Travis. 'Don't tense your fist till just before it lands.'

I throw the punch again, this time with a loose fist. *Thwack.*

'Nice,' says Travis. 'You can hear the difference, right? Now try rotating your fist just before impact, so it lands palm down.'

I punch again. *Smack.*

'Not bad,' says Travis. 'But do it faster. Reach out, make a fist, snap back. Imagine you're stealing a loaf of bread.'

I punch again. *Crack.*

'Again.'

Crack.

'Again.'

Crack.

'Who knew?' Travis chuckles. 'You're a natural bread thief. Now, listen up. That jab is going to be your most important weapon. It's the longest, fastest punch in your armory. Uses least energy, leaves you least vulnerable. Also, pretty much every combo starts with the jab. You're trying to stun your opponent just long enough for the bigger punches to land. Here, watch this.'

He stands side-on to the camera and throws five energetic jabs at an imaginary assailant.

'Very nice,' I say.

'One of the best jabs in New York,' mutters Travis. 'Everyone says so.'

TRAINING

Haven't written for two weeks. Still grounded. Still training.

Over the last two weeks I've been Skyping Travis almost every night. He teaches me how to move, how to shuffle, how to pivot on my feet. He puts me through drill after drill and chides me when I let my guard drop.

In return, I help Travis with his chess. I show him how to assess the strong and weak points in any position and devise a plan accordingly. I show him how to build a strong pawn structure, how to find the best outposts for knights and bishops, how to weave a mating net. I explain to him the difference between strategy and tactics and set him puzzles to improve both.

It bugs me when Travis doesn't listen to what I tell him, but he is making progress all the same. We train like maniacs and at the end of every training session, we kick back and dream of future men's and women's chessboxing glory.

'Bet I win a world title before you do,' I tell him one night.

'Wouldn't be so sure of that,' he laughs. 'I don't think they allow entrants via Skype.'

In this apartment, you never know when the next battle is going to erupt. Like tonight, for example. I'm in the middle of a boxing lesson when Mom comes into my room. I don't hear her knocking because I've got my earbuds in, but I suddenly see her out of the corner of my eye. She is leaning against the doorframe, cradling a large glass of gin, watching me punch the bag. She can't see my phone on the shelf. She has no idea I'm being coached.

I take out my earbuds and turn to face her. 'Hey, Mom.'

She scowls at the heavy bag, still swaying slightly on its chain. 'Stupid thing,' she says.

'It's not stupid. Dad bought it for me.'

'We bought it so you could increase your stamina for chess games, not so you could take up actual boxing.' Mom curls her lip in disgust. 'It's barbaric, that's what it is. Hitting each other in the head until one of you can't stand up anymore. They should ban it.'

I take off my gloves and sit down on the edge of my bed. I've been expecting this conversation and now is as good a time as any. 'Boxing is banned in two countries, Mom. Do you know which ones?'

Mom swirls her gin in the glass. The ice cubes clink and rattle. 'Sweden?' she says at last. 'Norway?'

166

'North Korea and Iran.'

She doesn't pause to consider this, just blunders on regardless. 'They've got the right idea, those North Koreans. Did you know, a young man in Colorado died in the ring last week? It was on CNN.'

'It was on CNN because it's so freaking rare. Fifty times rarer than mountaineering deaths and a hundred times rarer than horse-racing deaths.'

'No need to raise your voice, Leah. Anyways, I'm not just talking about deaths, I'm talking about concussion. Head injury. Brain damage.'

'Similar rates to football,' I reply, 'but no one talks about banning NFL, do they?'

Mom scowls and takes another slug of her drink. 'P'raps they should,' she slurs. 'Do us all a favor, ban them both.'

'Right.' I look at her glass. 'You know what causes more brain damage than boxing and football put together, don't you, Mom?'

'Don't make this about me,' she snaps. 'Don't make this—'

She chokes on her words and escapes along the corridor, grunting and snuffling like a warthog. I shut the bedroom door and put my earbuds back in.

'You should go easy on her,' says Travis in my ear. 'She's worried about you.'

'Shut up, jock.' I unleash an almighty punch that makes the bag creak and groan on its chain. 'If I want advice on my family life, I'll ask for it.'

INSOMNIA

Two o'clock and I still can't sleep.

It's not the heat that's keeping me awake. It's guilt.

I hardly ever feel guilt, but I'm pretty sure that's what this is. I knew Mom was upset last night and I was completely indifferent. Even Travis called me out on it and he's got the emotional intelligence of Jar Jar Binks.

Travis doesn't know the half of it. I wasn't indifferent. I was glad to see her crying.

Why?

I don't know.

Because I don't want to be the only one in the house who still cries?

Because I still resent her for how she was with me after Dad died?

Because I'm a moral moron?

All of the above?

ACCIDENT AMY

Two fifteen and I'm still awake.

I'm thirsty so I get out of bed and go to the kitchen for a glass of water. When I put the light on, I'm amazed to see Mom sitting on the kitchen floor with her back against the refrigerator. Her eyes are red and puffy, like she's been crying for a long time.

When the light comes on, Mom jumps up way too fast, slipping on the vinyl floor and toppling over sideways like a patzer's king.

A few years ago we would have laughed at a pratfall like that. When I was little we used to cuddle up on the couch to watch the *George Lopez Show*, all three of us together. The character we loved best was the clumsy factory worker Accident Amy. Every time she stepped in a bucket or got scooped up by a forklift truck, Dad would laugh till he cried and that would set me and Mom off, and the couch would shake beneath us for minutes on end. Sometimes we even re-enacted Amy's accidents ourselves, just to keep on laughing.

No one's laughing now. Mom struggles to her knees, hides her face in her hands and bursts into tears. I want to go straight back to my bedroom and curl up in bed, but I can't leave her like this. I may be a moral moron but I'm not a monster.

I kneel in front of Mom on the floor, loop my arms around her neck and stay there awkwardly while she weeps into my chest.

'I miss your father,' she says.

'I know,' I whisper. 'I miss him too.'

We sit back against the fridge, side by side, staring straight ahead like zombies. Catharsis, that's what this is. The right shoulder of my WAKE ME WHEN I'M A UNICORN camisole clings to my skin, wet through with tears. Who would have thought that Mom had so much salt water in her?

She frowns at the dirt and fluff that surrounds us. 'I should sweep this floor tomorrow.'

'I'll do it,' I hear myself say.

She puts a hand on my knee, then quickly takes it off again. Probably felt me flinch. 'I talked to a child psychologist today,' she says.

'I'm not a child.'

'She's called Daphne Piano.'

'Dumb name.'

'She was very sweet, Leah. She wants to help you.'

'At what, eighty bucks an hour? I'll bet she wants to help me.'

Mom wipes her eyes on the sleeve of her sweatshirt. 'She has good reviews on her website.'

I don't reply to that last comment. It hangs in the air, diffusing its dumbness throughout the kitchen. From the street outside I hear the drunken clatter of high heels and warbled snatches of some corny Suki Jones song: *Your white hat fell in the dirt, your ham hands can't fix my hurt* . . .

'Two fifteen,' says Mom, squinting up at the clock. 'You should get some sleep.'

'Here's an idea,' I say. 'I'll have a session with Daphne Piano—'

'Thank you!'

'And then a lesson at the boxing gym straight after.'

'Absolutely not.'

I fill my glass and head for the door. 'Night, Mom,' I say. 'Give Dr Daphne a call in the morning. Tell her to jump in a lake.'

Like me, the great Bobby Fischer was always being told he should see a psychiatrist. Unlike me, the great Bobby Fischer probably needed one.

1. At nine years old he filled his school notebooks with pictures of severed heads.

2. At twelve years old he used to play friendly games of chess against his mentor, GM Reuben Fine. When Fine casually inquired how things were going at school, Bobby flipped out. He screamed, 'You've tricked me!' and never spoke to Fine again.

3. At fifteen he lost a game to Mikhail Tal in Yugoslavia. He stormed outside in a rage but naughty old Tal followed him, flapping his hands and calling, 'Cuckoo, cuckoo!' Bobby burst into tears, ran to his room and pretended to have developed a cold. His roommate Bent Larsen read him Tarzan and Mickey Mouse stories until he calmed down and carried on with the tournament.

4. Bobby was convinced the world would end in 1972. It didn't, but he did beat Boris Spassky that year to become World Champion.

5. He took apart every hotel room he stayed in, looking for CIA bugs.

6. He had a dentist remove his fillings, for fear that Soviet agents would use the metal to send disruptive radio signals to his brain. His hollow teeth rotted away slowly inside his head.

7. In spite of everyone advising him to see a psychiatrist, Bobby always refused. 'A psychiatrist ought to pay *me*,' he said, 'for the privilege of working on my brain.'

GOOD UMBRELLA

Coach comes around to our place just as much as when he was tutoring me, if not more. Mom seems to like him hanging around, but for me it's just plain weird. It's bad enough watching him playing Scrabble and snacking on beef jerky with his mouth open, but lately he's been telling me to call him Clint instead of Coach. No way. He doesn't even look like a Clint.

All Coach and I ever used to talk about was chess. That's what Mom paid him for. Now that we can't talk about chess we just stand around clicking our knuckles and making awkward chit-chat, like two ex-vampires trying not to talk about blood.

We don't talk about Dad, either, until one night I open the door to Coach and see him holding Dad's umbrella.

'Just bringing this back,' he mumbles, propping it in the corner. 'It was raining last night when I left, and your mom said . . .'

He leaves the sentence unfinished, but I won't let him off that easily. 'Mom said what?'

'She said I could borrow it.' He peers over my shoulder. 'Is she in?'

'That's Dad's umbrella.'

'It's a very good umbrella.'

'It's Dad's.'

'Yes.' Coach edges past me into the hallway. 'A real gust-buster. Your father sure knew what to look for in an umbrella. Steel frame, see, and good solid rivets to hold the ribs in place. Not like my umbrellas. Mine keep getting blown inside out. *We're too poor to buy cheap stuff*, that's what my old pop used to say, but do I learn? Heck, no. I keep buying the cheap ones.'

'Are you sleeping with my mom?'

'Nice grippy handle,' says Coach, pretending not to have heard. 'But of course you don't want to spend a fortune on an umbrella because let's face it you're going to end up leaving it in a bar or in a cab or on the subway or—'

'Are you sleeping with my—?'

'Leah, how dare you!' cries Mom, zooming along the hallway, brandishing her hair-straighteners in front of her.

'Hello, Joanne,' Coach mumbles. 'We were talking about umbrellas. And I was just going.'

'Horsefeathers,' says Mom. 'You'll stay for dinner. There's leftover meatloaf in the fridge.'

Mom wears her best dress, the emerald-green velour one with the sweetheart neckline. The microwaved meatloaf is dry and tasteless but Coach fills the silence by rabbiting on about how delicious it is. Mom is still furious about what I said to him, and I am still furious at the thought of him galumphing around Greenwich Village with Dad's umbrella.

At the end of the meal Mom gets up from the table to go to the bathroom. As she leaves the room, she skewers me with a fierce Be Nice Or Else glare.

I look out the window. The dark clouds have parted and the roof of the shed glows rust red in the evening sun. Coach stops fiddling with his fork and looks up at me with a strange frown.

'Your mother doesn't waddle,' he says.

'What?'

'I've been reading your blog, Leah. You kept using the word waddle. *Mom waddled toward me as if to hug me. Mom waddled into the donut shop.* That sort of thing. What's with all the waddling? It's factually incorrect as well as disrespectful. She's not even overweight.'

I sit there hardly breathing and my heart is pounding like mad. 'My blog, my choice of words,' I mumble.

'It's not just the waddling that bothers me, it's the way you make her out to be some kind of ogre who only cares about having a chess grandmaster for a daughter and doesn't love you for yourself. It's not true, Leah. Your mother's a fine woman and she loves you more than you could possibly imagine. She's been dealt a difficult hand and she's doing her best with it. All I'm saying is, you can't write stuff that isn't true and just put it out there for everyone to read.'

I look down at my hands. 'How did you find my blog?'

'I watched your video yesterday on chess.com. That blitz game against Roderick Wilde. Someone in the comments section linked back to your blog.'

'I see.'

'And that's another thing, Leah.' Coach gathers up the plates and carries them to the sink. 'Blitz is bad for your chess. If you persist in playing nothing but blitz, you'll forget how to calculate long lines and your FIDE rating will go through the floor.'

I don't have to listen to any more of this. I push my chair away from the table without a word and head for the door.

'Be that as it may,' Coach continues, 'some of those moves you played against Wilde made the hairs stand up on the back of my neck. Best game I've seen in years.'

My hand is on the door handle. I stop and look back.

Coach snaps on a pair of dishwashing gloves. 'I'm actually jealous you spotted queen to g3, Leah. If you'd done that in a tournament, it would have won a brilliancy prize, no questions asked, but to do it in a blitz game is more than a brilliancy. It's a miracle. All the guys at the Manhattan Club are talking about it.' He laughs and shakes his head. 'I would never even have considered Qg3 in that position. Maybe you were struck by lightning as a baby or bitten by a spider or something.'

I moisten my lips. 'I was well taught,' I say.

Mom comes back in and looks straight at Coach to see if I've upset him yet. He's got meatloaf gravy on his shirt but seems otherwise normal, cheerful even, so she grins like a crazy woman and suggests tapioca pudding for dessert.

Coach starts washing dishes and gabbling about tapioca being his favorite. I make an excuse and retreat to my room. Nothing good can come of a dessert that looks like a bowlful of hummingbird eyeballs in cream sauce. Besides, I'm not in the mood for dessert.

Back in my room I fill my ears with *The Resurrection* and beat the living daylights out of the punchbag. I punch with a loose fist, clenching and twisting before impact, stealing loaf after loaf after loaf after loaf of stale, weeviled bread.

At nine o'clock Mom knocks on my door and opens it a few inches. 'Clint went home,' she says.

'Good.' I whack the bag with a straight fist, feeling the impact all the way along my arm into my shoulder socket.

'And for your information,' she adds, 'he and I have never been together, not in that way. We're friends. Perhaps one day we will be something more than friends. If that bothers you, I'm sorry. But there comes a time when the grief begins to lift and you feel you can move on.'

Move on. Ha. How brisk that sounds. How resolute. *Moving on up, nothing can stop me . . .*

'Besides,' Mom adds brightly, 'it does us good to have some male company.'

Some male company. As if that's all Dad was to us. A token Y chromosome at the kitchen table.

I can still see Mom out of the corner of my eye. I keep expecting her to say goodnight and go to bed, but she stands there for ages, watching me pound the bag.

'I told Clint you wanted to take up boxing,' she says at last. 'I felt sure he'd agree with me about it.'

'And?'

'He said boxing instils character and discipline.'

I stop punching the bag and turn to face her. 'Go on.'

'I don't know,' she sighs. 'Perhaps he's right.'

'So I can join a boxing gym?'

Fear and resolve chase each other across Mom's face. 'Two conditions,' she says at last. 'First, you get a job. A proper job, not hustling in the park. Second, you book ten grief therapy sessions with Daphne Piano.'

JOB-HUNTING

A proper job. Easier said than done.

My first port of call is *Gonuts Donuts*. Randal Johnson has had plenty of time to cool down and I figure he'll jump at the chance of hiring someone who already knows the ropes.

Ronda is serving on the front counter when I go in. As soon as she sees me she claps her hands and squeals in excitement.

When I tell her I want my job back, she shows me the STAFF WANTED notice on the counter where it was before. 'My father's in his office,' she says, crossing her fingers on both hands. 'Make sure you act real humble. Keep telling him how sorry you are. Good luck!'

What follows is the shortest job interview ever. Turns out that not even a truckful of sorries is enough to mollify the donut chief.

'What happened?' gasps Ronda, when I return to the counter thirty seconds later.

'Your father said he wouldn't hire me if I were the last person on Earth.'

Ronda's face falls, then brightens again. 'That would be true of anyone,' she says. 'If there was only one person left on Earth, he would need to sell them donuts, not hire them.'

I go around the back of the counter and give Ronda an awkward half-hug. 'I've missed you,' I tell her.

'I've missed you too,' she says, and she's looking at me like, Who is this person?

LIVER

On my way out of *Gonuts Donuts*, I run into Kit.

'Hey!' he exclaims. 'Nathan said he saw you go in here. I told him it couldn't be you.'

'It was me. Is me. Mom let me out.'

We drift along Greene Street and through the east gate into

the park. The sun through the trees casts dappled light across the sidewalk.

'It's good to see you,' says Kit.

'Good to see you too.' It's the right thing to say and it's also the truth.

Kit seems cheerful. He says the Poisoned Pawns are playing harder than ever, making the most of the time they have left before the city's gambling laws get updated. Then he asks what I've been up to, so I tell him about my Skype boxing lessons with Travis.

Kit kicks a rock into the long grass. 'You got the hots for this Travis creature?'

'No!'

'You're giving him chess lessons.'

'That's the deal.'

'I'll bet he sets the board up wrong half the time.'

'He's doing fine. Can we talk about something else?'

We sit down on the grass on the other side of the path from Larry the birdman. He is on his usual bench with his head, shoulders, arms and lap all covered in pigeons. There must be at least fifty of them all over him and on the ground as well. In the middle of that flurry of beaks and feathers, Larry sits content and motionless, a smiling, bird-strewn Buddha.

'Look how they trust him,' whispers Kit. 'I've tried sitting on that bench myself a few times. Eyes closed, arms out, placid as you like. The birds don't even come near me.'

'I guess trust takes time,' I say. 'Here's a question for you, Kit. Who was that guy in the myth who had a bird pecking his insides all the time?'

'Prometheus,' replies Kit, quick as a flash. 'He stole fire from the gods and his punishment was to be chained to a rock with an eagle pecking at his liver. Every night his liver grew back magically so the eagle always had fresh meat to peck. *The rock, the vulture, and the chain, all that the proud can feel of pain.*'

'Shakespeare?'

'Byron.'

I lie back on the grass and close my eyes. 'You know what?' I whisper. 'That's kind of how I've felt since my dad died. Every time I think my insides are healing up, the grief comes back and pecks 'em all up again.'

'Sucks to be you,' says Kit.

I open my eyes and look at him to see if he's making fun of me. He's not.

'You want to hear something gross?' I say.

'Always.' He lies down next to me.

'My dad died because his body ate itself.'

Kit's body goes really still and tense, like he's holding his breath.

'Pancreatic juices,' I murmur. 'They're supposed to digest your food, right? But when my dad got sick his pancreatic juices leaked into his abdomen and started digesting his actual insides.'

Kit reaches out and takes my hand. He holds it tight and says nothing.

'Mom and I weren't with him when he died. We were at a chess tournament in Rhode Island. I was playing chess like you wouldn't believe. Razor sharp. Totally focussed. Winning all my games. And whilst I was doing that, Dad was slipping in and out of consciousness, delirious with pain and meds. If we'd been with him, we could have kept him strong, but we weren't and he died.'

'How long ago did this happen?' Kit's voice is a whisper, like he's in church or something.

'Two years, three months and twenty-one days. I should be over it by now, shouldn't I? I should be moving on with my life. Making new friends. Working on my chess. Making Dad proud by becoming the first ever female World Chess Champion. But instead of doing all that I'm chained to a rock getting pecked to bits. And when anyone gets close to me I make damn sure they get their ass pecked too. My boyfriend,

Sergey? He was with me at the Rhode Island tournament and I broke up with him soon afterward because every time I looked at him I remembered how I wasn't there when Dad died. And my only non-chess friend, Stephanie? I told her I hated her because her dad was still alive and mine wasn't. Haven't seen her since. That's what grief does, Kit. It makes you lash out at people. Drive them away. I've got this theory that they should build huge colonies for all the people who've lost someone. Great long rows of rocks and chains, and the flesh-eating eagle can go from one rock to the next like some ugly-ass GM playing a forty-board simul.'

'Sheesh,' Kit breathes. 'I don't know what to say.' He props himself up on one elbow and looks at me. Or rather, his straight eye is looking at me. The wonky one is looking away over my shoulder somewhere. He's got tears in both of them, the big softie.

'Let go of my hand,' I tell him. 'You're cutting off my blood supply.'

AD

That night over dinner I tell Mom and Clint about my failed visit to Gonuts Donuts.

'His loss,' sniffs Mom.

'Here's an idea,' says Clint. 'Why not offer chess tuition?

184

You've been quite the celebrity in chess circles since the Wilde video went viral, so you may as well cash in. Post an advert on the coaching forum at chess.com. You'll have a ton of responses, I guarantee it.'

It's not a bad idea, so I grab my phone and draft an ad:

COULD YOUR CHILD BE THE NEXT BOBBY FISCHER?

Leah Baxter aka Park Girl, an international master with a FIDE rating of 2470 and a reputation for sensational attacking chess, is taking on a limited number of students.

After a year of tuition with Leah your child will be able to:

- understand the principles behind their favorite openings

- assess any position and formulate a plan

- spot electrifying tactical combinations that will wow spectators and win brilliancy prizes

- play out any endgame with the ruthless accuracy of a killer robot

- leave any opponent crushed and bleeding on the chessboard

Clint looks over my shoulder and bursts out laughing. 'Kind of aggressive, isn't it?'

'Of course,' I say. 'That's what the green-room parents want. They want their little Imogen to sit down at the tournament chessboard, shake hands nicely with little Jasper, start the clocks and then, you know, rip little Jasper's heart out of his chest and eat it.'

'Good point,' says Clint. 'Post the ad and see what happens.'

THEODORE

Theodore Inigo Croft is seven years old and he lives in one of the elegant row houses on West 87th Street just off Riverside Drive. His parents Charles and Mary Croft run a successful greetings card business and are hardly ever at home, so Theodore and his younger sister Vanessa have a nanny to look after them. The nanny drops them off at school, picks them up, cooks their dinner and plays board games with them: Settlers, Carcassonne, Pandemic, Clue, Ticket to Ride, Mastermind, Boggle, Hungry Hippos.

Much as Theodore enjoys Hungry Hippos, his greatest love is chess. His father is the first person to respond to my coaching ad, so I arrange to visit them at home the following Wednesday.

When I arrive at the house, Teddy's nanny greets me at the door and shows me into the living room. There they are, arranged on the couch like some dumbass studio portrait: kids in the middle, parents on either end, two russet-colored basset hounds reclining at their feet.

Charles and Mary leap up, pump my hand and ask me a bunch of newbie questions so infuriating I want to scream and run away. *How many openings should Theodore master? How many moves ahead will he be able to calculate? How long before they promote him to Board 1 in the school chess team? Will chess make him a good mathematician? Businessman? Politician? General? Artist?*

I explain why their questions are impossible to answer and they nod earnestly like they understand. Even little Vanessa is nodding at me like a bobble-head doll.

'Theodore wants to win the School Cup,' says Charles. 'No second-grader ever won it before. I told him you would teach him some nifty openings that will fox the older kids.'

'The most important thing is not to pressure him,' I say, and both parents flinch like I've accused them of cannibalism.

Then comes the grand unveiling of the family chess set. Mary dims the lights while her husband fetches the chess set and places it reverently in the middle of the mahogany dining table. The translucent onyx board is illuminated from beneath and it glows majestically in the darkened room. Thirty-two cut-glass chessmen glint and sparkle on the board, scattering prismatic rainbows in all directions. One of the basset hounds raises its head and growls at the irradiated intruders.

'What do you think?' whispers Mary.

'Dumbest thing I've ever seen,' I reply. 'You've even set it up wrong. The bottom right square should be white.'

Charles carries the heirloom forlornly back to its cupboard and Theodore scoots off to find a cheap plastic chess set that we can use for our tuition. While they are gone Mary gives me some serious side eye and little Vanessa cavorts around the room with a pilfered cut-glass knight, singing *Horsey, horsey, don't you stop.*

Ten minutes later Theodore and I are alone at the table and ready to start our lesson.

'Sorry about my family,' he mutters. 'They mean well.'

'Don't be sorry, Theodore. You're lucky to have them.'

The small boy nods and wipes his nose on his hand. 'My friends call me Teddy,' he says.

DAPHNE

Daphne Piano's office is just off 7th Avenue. She has a tiny bespectacled face framed by an enormous mop of long dark curls. Looks like a mouse in a mulberry bush.

She hands me a mug of hot chocolate and tries to soften me up with warm smiles and inane questions about music and hobbies. You would think a woman called Piano would have some awareness of classical music, but when I tell her I like

Mahler, she thinks I'm talking about Mala off *America's Got Talent*. And when I mention chess she nods a little too warmly. Mom has already briefed her on my unique brand of crazy.

'You must be very clever indeed,' Daphne enthuses.

'That's right.' I flash her my looniest grin. 'Insanely clever.'

Daphne tells me we're going to be doing 'grief work' in these sessions, which sounds sprightly and challenging, like a mud run or a firewalk. Complete the course and skip off into the sunset.

'We'll be basing our grief work on this book,' she says, passing it to me.

My heart sinks. *The Five Stages of Grief.* I stare at the index, its neatly ordered sections corresponding to five neat stages.

1. Shattering
2. Withdrawal
3. Internalizing
4. Anger
5. Lifting

'Why are there tooth marks on the cover?' I hold the book up to the light, so she can see. 'Somebody got so mad at this book they actually bit it. Was it you?'

Daphne recoils. 'I don't bite books.'

'Did you lend it to somebody?'

'I've lent it to lots of people.' She forces a smile. 'Would you like to borrow it?'

'No.'

'Why not?' Daphne is still smiling, but there is an edge of challenge in her tone.

What should I tell her? That I read the *Five Stages* online three months after Dad died? That I believed it and derived hope from it and went through the stages all the way to Lifting and then one day right out of a blue sky flipped back to Shattering all over again? That my belief in the five stages died a slow painful death just like Dad? That I'm going to write my own book, *The Five Rages of Death*, consisting of ninety per cent cuss words?

I don't feel ready to tell her any of that. Not today, anyways. I shrug my shoulders and press the skin between my thumb and forefinger until it hurts.

BERT

As soon as my appointment with Daphne is over I take the subway to Hell's Kitchen and meet Travis down by the river.

'How you doing?' he asks.

'Fine.' I haven't told him I'm seeing a shrink and I don't intend to.

Travis smiles. 'It's good to see you in person for a change. You look good in high def.'

He's flirting with me. I guess I should feel flattered. Plenty of girls would think Travis quite a catch.

We walk to the boxing gym, a converted car park underneath an apartment block in the sort of neighborhood where your car isn't safe. BERT'S GYM reads the sign above the door, and then in smaller letters TRAINING BOXERS SINCE 1951.

The stairwell reeks of sweat and leather, and when we get into the gym itself the smell is so pungent it makes me gag. Not at all like the sterile hotel gyms I'm used to.

'Proper spit and sawdust boxing gym,' says Travis, reading my expression. 'No air conditioning. No towels. No changing rooms. Just weights, punchbags and the best coach in all of New York.'

The gym echoes with the squeak of shoes, the thud of bags, the slap of ropes and the fierce exhalations of people working out. Raised up in the middle of the room stands the ring itself, a shrine to strength and skill. Right now a couple of kids are bouncing around in it, pummeling the mitted hands of a frowning coach. The coach has silver hair and there is something funny about his right eyelid. It kind of droops.

'That's Bert,' says Travis, nodding toward the old man. 'Come on up, I'll introduce you.'

We climb up onto the apron and duck through the ropes into the ring itself. I've never set foot in a real boxing ring but already I feel a tingle of *déjà-vu*, like this is where I've always belonged.

'Bert, this is Leah,' Travis is saying. 'She wants to learn to box.'

'She's come to the right place.' Bert is still holding up the mitts for the kids to punch, but he is looking at me with his droopy right eye and it's like he can see into my soul.

TRAINING

After every session with Daphne I take the subway to Hell's Kitchen and walk to Bert's stinky gym. There's no getting used to that foul smell, however long I spend there. It gets into the gloves, the bags, the floor, the walls and even your skin. They should paint over that 1951 brag on the sign above the door, and replace it with: 'Hold your nose, all ye who enter here'.

I have traced the epicenter of the smell to the big plastic glove bin under the boxing ring. That thing reeks! If you don't bring your own boxing gloves you have to borrow some from the glove bin, so make sure you get a good lungful of air before you lift the lid. And don't spend too long trying on different sizes or you'll wind up semi-conscious on the floor. *What's up, dude, you get dinged by Wladimir Klitschko? No, bro, I just opened the glove bin.*

This is my training routine at Bert's Gym:

1. Fifteen-minute run around Hell's Kitchen
2. Fifteen minutes of circuit training: squats, dips, push-ups, chin-ups, lunges.
3. Fifteen minutes on Jacob's Ladder
4. Eight minutes on the punchbags
5. Eight-minute cooldown
6. Repeat

The worst bit of the routine (apart from opening the glove bin) is climbing Jacob's Ladder. Bert calls it a fitness machine but torture machine would be more accurate. Imagine a runged treadmill sloping upward at a 45-degree angle, and then imagine that the rungs move down at the same speed that you're climbing up, and then imagine you have to strap yourself onto that thing and bust your ass for a full fifteen minutes.

When I'm on the ladder I pretend that I'm Ethan Hunt climbing the Burj Khalifa, and also that I'm not afraid of heights.

After three minutes my muscles are burning and my pretending goes out the window.

After ten minutes I no longer know my own name.

After fifteen minutes I want nothing more than to crawl into a deep dark ditch and die.

But instead of dying in a ditch I have to stagger over to the punchbags and start boxing. There are twelve punchbags in Bert's gym, ranging from speed bags to heavy bags to gigantic body bags that only the strongest punchers can move. I alternate between a speed bag for hand-eye coordination and a heavy bag for stamina.

I stand in front of the heavy bag, a sweaty, exhausted mess. Sometimes Bert appears at my shoulder and nags me while I punch. *Keep your wrists straight. Elbows tight. Faster now. Show that thing who's boss. Stop holding your breath! That's better. Make it shake all over, like it's having a seizure. You're doing good. Stay strong.*

Everyone's always telling me to stay strong, but something about the way Bert says it makes me actually believe it's possible.

SYDNEY

During one soul-sapping session on Jacob's Ladder, I hear a voice close by that isn't Bert or Travis.

'Lighten up! You're stepping way too hard.'

I look, and there beside me in a pristine white tracksuit stands Sydney 'Shock and Awe' Campbell.

194

'You're stepping too hard,' she repeats. 'Focus on the balls of your feet and tread real light. Tippy-tappy, tippy-tappy, tippy-tappy, like that.'

I knew that Sydney trained at Bert's gym and I had been looking forward to meeting her, but right now I'm not in the mood for advice.

'Thanks,' I pant. 'I'll do it my way, if you don't mind.'

'Your way's no good.'

'And your chess is no good.' Immediately I want to grab my words out of the air and cram them back into my mouth, but it's too late.

'What did you say to me?'

'Nothing.'

The Jacob's Ladder strap goes suddenly taut, yanking me backward off the machine. I sprawl on the gym mats at the boxer's feet.

Sydney bunches the strap in her hands, then wrenches it again to pull me to my feet. 'You got something to say about my chess?'

'Okay.' I unbuckle my waistband to put an end to her puppet-on-a-string routine. 'I saw you play at the Elephant Club, and you know what? If Frank Marshall wasn't already dead, your version of the Marshall Attack would have finished him off for sure.'

The chessboxer takes a step toward me. She is only a couple of inches taller than me but it seems like a lot more. 'I'm going to give you the benefit of the doubt and assume you don't know who I am,' she snarls. 'I'm a three-time US Army chess champion.'

'Congratulations! Were there no other entrants?'

She comes closer. I can smell the musk from her workout. 'I'll play you at chess any time you like, smiler, and I'll kick your ass so bad it'll end up on your shoulders.'

'Sounds fun. Let's have a game right now.'

'We got no board.'

'Only patzers need a board. Come on, you be White.'

'What?'

'Fine, I'll be White. Pawn d4. Your move.'

Her brow furrows. 'd5.'

'e4.'

'd takes.'

'Knight c3.'

'Knight f6.'

'f3.'

Sydney scowls. 'I ain't got time for this.'

'Don't tell me you've lost track of the position already? Come on, it's your move.'

'Listen, Flat-ass. I'm going to close my eyes and I'm going to count to ten. If you're still standing in front of me when I open my eyes, I'm going to lay you out so cold that when you wake up your clothes will be out of fashion.'

As soon as she closes her eyes, I run for the door.

Okay, writing it down now, I'm embarrassed. Why do I have to be so obnoxious?

THE DIFFICULT QUESTION

'Today I'm going to ask you to do something very difficult,' says Daphne. 'I want you to tell me about your father's death.'

My fingers tighten on the arms of the chair. 'No.'

High up in the corner of the room a cranefly flails. I count its legs. *One. Two. Three. Four. Five. Six. Seven.*

'Why do you keep doing that?' asks Daphne.

'Doing what?'

'That.' She points at my hand. 'Squeezing the skin between your thumb and fingers.'

'I read it in a magazine. It's supposed to stop you crying.'

'Does it work?'

'Yes.' I glance up at the disabled cranefly, which wiggles its seven legs accusingly at me. 'Sometimes.'

'Thanks for the tip.' Daphne smiles. 'Tell me, Leah, do you journal?'

'Yes.'

'Do you ever write about your father's death?'

'No.'

'Have a go sometime. Don't worry, I promise I won't ask to read anything you write.'

STONES

Are you ready, laptop dear? The following posts are going to make your motherboard short-circuit.

Just over two years ago Dad started getting pains in his tummy. His doctor said it was gallstones. *Nothing to worry about*, said the doctor, *but you probably ought to have your gallbladder removed.*

It was a simple, routine operation. So simple that a junior doctor did the surgery, and so routine that she got careless and dropped a couple of the stones into Dad's bile duct without realizing it. When Dad woke up after the operation, the pain was worse than ever. *Acute pancreatitis*, they said. *Nothing to worry about, but you will have to stay in hospital a few more days.*

There was a tournament on Rhode Island that week. We'd already paid the entrance fee and were all set to travel down there. Coach reckoned I had a good chance of winning it, so Dad insisted I go ahead and play. *Nothing to worry about*, he croaked. The hospital were giving him fluids and pain relief and he would start feeling better soon, he was sure of it. On my way out of the ward, he called me back. *Leah*, he whispered in my ear, *I'd open game one with the Kasparov Gambit if I were you. That'll fox 'em.*

Rhode Island was a blast. Mom and I had a room on the first floor of the hotel with sliding doors that opened onto the hotel swimming pool. I swam, I ran and I played the best chess of my life. On the first day I won all my games, even with the black pieces. I phoned Dad to tell him the news and he sounded weak but cheerful. *Well done, champ*, he said.

That night I hung out by the pool with my boyfriend Sergey. We practiced rook-pawn endgames on a tiny magnetic chess set and the loser of each game had to do a belly flop off the diving board. When Sergey's abs were too sore for any more belly flops, we took it in turns to do impressions of top ten grandmasters, laughing like loons as we tried to guess each other's impressions.

Afterward we sat by the pool with our legs dangling in the water. Sergey leaned toward me and cocked his head on one side like a puppy pleading for a snack. I laughed at his expression, and when I stopped laughing we kissed. I felt happy and excited, like a whole new world was opening up to me.

On the second day of the tournament, I won another two games and went four points clear at the top of the leaderboard. And then it happened. Eight moves into my Round 6 game, Mom came flying into the playing hall with a coffee stain all down her blouse. I was up out of my seat before she even reached the table. *Your father is in intensive care*, she said. *We need to go to him, Leah.*

Manhattan is only three hours away from Rhode Island but the drive that afternoon seemed to last forever, and then it took forever to find a parking space at the hospital, and then even the elevator took forever to arrive. We got to the Intensive Care Unit at 7.17 p.m. and were met by an old nurse with hairs on her chin.

Instead of taking us to see Dad, she told us to sit down. *I'm so sorry*, she said, and I didn't hear anything after that because I was clinging to Mom and she was clinging to me and we were deaf and blind with shock.

SEEING DAD

They did not let me see him at first. Too distressing, they said. But I refused to leave the hospital until they relented.

The nurse with the hairy chin unlocked the viewing room and stood aside. Mom came in with me, even though she'd already seen him. The corpse on the table was still wearing a hospital gown. The legs were covered by a gray sheet and the face was jaundiced and swollen, like a yellowing football.

'Hello, Dad,' I sobbed.

Hello champ, he didn't say.

I kissed my fingers and pressed them to his cheek. 'Why is he so cold?' I asked.

'He's been in the fridge,' the nurse said.

He's been in the fridge. I was shocked by the everydayness of the words. *Dad's been in the fridge and he's finished all the orange juice.*

EARLY DAYS

No one tells you how exhausting grief is. I mean physically exhausting, like running a marathon or canoeing in white water. Bruising too. You feel it through your whole body, like you've run full speed into a brick wall.

In the days after Dad died I used to fall asleep mid-afternoon and then wake in the middle of the night feeling like I couldn't breathe, like there was something pressing down on my chest. Mom suffered too. She kept getting these weird shooting pains on the right side of her stomach. She went to see a doctor. The diagnosis was – I'm not kidding – sympathy pains. Mom's brain was simulating pancreatic pain because that's what killed Dad. If that's not messed up, I don't know what is.

Dad's sister Dolores came to stay with us. She helped us organize the funeral. We couldn't afford a burial plot in New York but we got one at Grasslands Cemetery in New Jersey. Mom messaged all our friends and relatives to tell them the place and time. She composed the message slooooowly using just one finger, and then tapped SEND TO ALL.

Jack's funeral is at Grasslands Cemetery New Jersey next Thursday 2 p.m. LOL

When I told Mom what LOL stands for, she got so mad I wished I hadn't. Eventually she calmed down and sent everyone a second message to apologize and explain. She'd thought it meant Lots of Love.

Grasslands Cemetery should have been called Mudlands Cemetery or maybe Weedlands Cemetery. We stood there in the pouring rain, me and Mom, surrounded by a huddle of uncles, aunts, cousins and friends, as well as a few of Dad's university colleagues – 'the beards', I call them. One of the beards, a guy called Geoff Eggers with a bald spot the size of South Dakota, was carrying a big old laptop. Mom had given permission for him to livestream the graveside ceremony to those at the university unable to attend.

The worst thing about the ceremony was not being able to tell Dad about all the dumb stuff that happened. *Poor you*, he would have said. *All those gray-faced undertakers and that priest with the too-tight collar, and Aunt Dolores slowly sinking into the turf in her stiletto heels. And that raccoon in the grave. Poor you!*

That's right, a raccoon in the grave. The hole had been dug the previous day and the racoon must have come along in the night and fallen into it. When we arrived with the coffin-bearers, there it was with its bushy tail and cute black mask, rushing to and fro at the bottom of the hole, chirruping indignantly.

No one took charge so we just stood in the rain with Dad's coffin, gazing into the grave. I wanted to jump down there and lift the poor creature out, but Mom told me not to. She said it would bite me and give me rabies.

Eventually one of the undertakers phoned the gravedigger to come and deal with it. We had to wait another twenty minutes for him to show up. You'd have thought Geoff Eggers would have stopped the livestream, but he just stood there with his umbrella over his laptop giving a dumbass running commentary on the creature's antics. *Won't you look at that now, folks, the little varmint is standing up on his hind legs with his little paws together. Looks for all the world like he's praying.*

Dad's coffin was made of cardboard. He was really into eco-friendly living so we figured it was what he would have wanted. Sure made us anxious, though, watching that cardboard coffin lid darkening in the rain. *Don't worry*, the funeral director said. *Cardboard coffins can withstand at least thirty minutes of heavy rain before they start to collapse.*

I imagined the gravedigger would bring some kind of special raccoon catching kit – a net on a pole or something – but when he finally arrived he had nothing but a scout rifle and a box of ammo. Me and my cousin Rachel begged him not to shoot but he wouldn't listen. He shot into the hole six times, then jumped in to retrieve the body. *Standard procedure*, he said.

Once the raccoon was gone, everything happened very fast. The coffin-bearers lowered the soggy coffin into the grave. I threw a rose on top of it. The fat-necked priest said a few words but he kept calling Dad 'John' (the name on the death certificate) instead of Jack (which everyone knew him as). And even though I didn't want to, I kept glancing back at the gravedigger's truck with that dead raccoon slung in the back, wondering what he was going to do with it.

Geoff Eggers livestreamed every minute of the ceremony and his final sign-off was jawdroppingly dumb. *That was Jack Baxter's burial, folks. I'm going to switch this thing off now. Thank you for watching.*

THINGS PEOPLE SAID TO ME AFTER THE BURIAL

1. I know just how you feel

2. You're doing so well

3. Chin up, buttercup

4. Stay strong

5. At least you and your mom still have each other

6. A vacation, that's what you need

7. Clever man, your father. Did I tell you about the time he came over to help me wire the tortoise switch on my model railroad?

8. You'll get over it.

Two weeks after the funeral, Mom drove me to New Jersey so that we could visit Dad's grave. We spent the morning pulling weeds and tending flowers, making everything neat and tidy.

At midday Mom went to buy lunch. As soon as she was out of earshot I did something I really regret. I sat down on Dad's gravestone and started hollering at him. *Stupid, selfish man! If you'd wanted to hang on, you could have done. You wanted to get away from us, didn't you? You left us because you didn't love us.*

I stopped, terrified by the ferocity of my own feelings, and then I looked up and saw the old gravedigger sitting silently under the trees watching me. So I hollered at him as well. *Murderer!* I yelled. *You could have saved that raccoon, but you couldn't resist the chance to jerk off that stupid gun of yours, could you? You should be in jail, you trigger-happy old nitwomble.*

Nitwomble. That's what I called him. It's not even a word.

Mom came back with two bottles of root beer and some cheese and tuna sandwiches. She sat down next to Dad's grave and laid the food between us.

'So peaceful,' she said. 'It's like he's right here with us. We should do this again soon, don't you think?'

'Did you write anything about your father's death?' Daphne asks.

'Yes.'

'Did you find it helpful?'

'No.'

Daphne takes off her glasses, cleans them with a tiny cloth and puts them back on. 'Your mom says you are experiencing self-sabotage.'

'I lost a couple of chess games. It happens.'

'Probably nothing, then.'

We sit there looking at each other. The clock ticks.

'If you were, though . . .'

'I'm not.'

'If you were, it wouldn't be uncommon. Bereavement shakes our stability, Leah. It dispels our illusion of being in control. When we lose someone close to us, insecurity and self-doubt creep in. We start thinking the death is somehow our fault and that we deserve to be punished in some way. Or we start believing we're under some sort of curse. *Bad things always happen to me*, we say, and before we know it we are at war with our own unconscious mind.'

'I'm not at war with my unconscious mind.'

'Of course not.' Daphne brushes a swathe of frizzy hair behind one ear. 'You would have noticed if you were, because you would have started to short-change yourself in all sorts of ways. The cyclist stops riding because he might fall off his bike. The writer stops writing because she no longer believes in the value of her words. The chess player . . .' An embarrassed smile plays around her lips.

'Go on.'

'The chess player starts moving way too fast. She's going to lose anyway, so why not get it over with? Like all self-sabotage, it's a safety mechanism to protect her from disappointment.'

She's trying so hard, I almost feel sorry for her. 'Yes, maybe that's it,' I say, just to get her off my back.

But Daphne doesn't get off my back. She has smelled blood and now there is no stopping her. She leans forward in her chair, coming in for the kill. 'What happened to your dad was not your fault, Leah.'

'I know.' I squeeze my hand. 'Why would it be?'

'It was not your fault,' she repeats.

'I know.'

'You deserve to be happy.'

'Yes.'

'You will succeed in all sorts of ways, and live a happy, fulfilled life.'

'Sure.'

'And if you ever take up chess again, you will sit at that board and play the most clear-minded, deliberate, powerful chess of your life.'

'What about chessboxing?'

'What?'

'Will I be good at chessboxing?'

'Indeed you will.' Daphne's eyes have gone glassy. 'You will succeed at whatever you put your hand to.'

'Snake-charming?'

'Whatever you put your hand to.'

'Bank robbery?'

Daphne clenches her jaw and looks up at the clock on the wall. 'I think that's enough for today,' she says.

GUARD

When I finish my workout, I like to sit on a stool beside the ring and watch the boxers spar. Beginners paw each other like clumsy kittens, bouncing back and forth, terrified of getting hit. Seasoned fighters are different. They attack each other like wild cats, their grunts and hisses echoing around the four walls of the gym.

Watching the experienced boxers gives me goose bumps and makes me long to be in the ring myself. I keep asking Bert but he keeps saying no. He says I'm still not ready. Says I need to work on my technique. The closest I get to sparring is when Bert calls me into the ring to pummel his mitted hands. He shows me how to move forward and backward with a step-drag motion, and he keeps reminding me to bring my hand back to my face after each punch.

Imagine a piece of elastic between your wrist and your left cheek, he says. *Punch, snap back, punch, snap back. Never let your guard drop.*

ALL IS WELL

Daphne tells me to imagine that Dad is sitting in the next room. She tells me to imagine that he is close to us, just through the wall. He can hear everything we are saying.

'Listen,' says Daphne, cupping a hand to her rainforest of hair. 'He's speaking. He's saying your name. What's that he's saying? He's saying *All is Well.*'

'No, he's not. He's dead.'

Daphne nods solemnly. 'This is an imaginative exercise which some people find helpful. It's easier if you close your eyes.'

I close my eyes just to stop her talking, but she doesn't stop talking. She keeps saying, 'All is well' in a soft trancelike voice that sounds nothing like Dad. I want to reach out and punch her in the All is Well, because the fact is, all is not well. Death is a horrible business and eighty-dollar-an-hour mind games don't make it any better.

'What do you feel, Leah?' Daphne whispers.

'I feel numb.' I open my eyes. 'I feel like it would be better if you said your "All is well" in a sarcastic tone of voice.'

'You want me to say it sarcastically?'

'That would be more like Dad. Our car broke down on the way to a chess tournament one time, and Dad started saying "Don't Panic!" in an ironic *Hitchhiker's Guide to the Galaxy* kind of way. Perhaps it would be better if we changed the phrase to *I'm Dead but Don't Panic.*'

'*I'm Dead but Don't Panic?*' Daphne sounds unsure. This isn't in any of her textbooks.

'No, even more sarcastic than that. Say it in a high-pitched singsong kind of voice.'

'I don't think that would be helpful.'

'I think perhaps it would.'

I close my eyes again. There is a long silence and then suddenly Daphne chirrups, 'I'm Dead but Don't Panic!' and I burst out laughing and crying at the same time, and I hate myself for letting my guard drop.

SPARRING

One afternoon I'm in the ring punching Bert's mitts when he suddenly lowers his hands and tells me to open my mouth.

'What?'

'Open your mouth,' he repeats. 'As wide as you can. Good. Now close it again. And open. And close. And open. And close. And move your jaw in a circle clockwise. Counter-clockwise. Clockwise. Counter-clockwise.'

With a thrill of excitement, I realize what this is. This is me warming up my jaw. This is preparation for sparring.

Sure enough, Bert passes me a mouthguard and some protective headgear. 'Joshua!' he shouts. 'Get on up here.'

A gangly kid with buck teeth appears from behind a punchbag and trots toward the ring. He ducks under the ropes, nods at Bert and smiles uncertainly at me.

'Round one,' says Bert. 'Off you go.'

We circle each other with our gloves up to our faces. Step, drag, step, drag, around and around we go. He's nervous, this kid, and I can't help wondering if it's his first time as well. I throw one jab, then another, then another. All three glance harmlessly off his gloves. *Get your jab landing first*, that's what Bert always says. *If your jab doesn't land, nothing else will.*

I bend my knees and throw a jab to Joshua's ribcage. I try to follow up with a right cross but he pivots to one side and wheels away from me. I go after him, jabbing hard and fast, but somehow his arms and gloves are blocking everything I throw.

'Stop backing up and start hitting her!' Bert yells. 'She needs to learn.'

The kid stops backing away and starts hitting me. He peppers my face and chin with gangly jabs, not so much painful as humiliating.

I snort in anger and launch a straight right into thin air. Big mistake. A powerful left hook comes out of nowhere and knocks me sideways. I guess I was wrong. This is not his first time.

'Raise your guard, Leah,' Bert yells. 'Get your head moving!'

I scowl and stumble forward like Frankenstein's monster. I don't even know where my opponent is anymore but he is hitting me with shot after shot and I'm landing none of my own. I feel like I'm drowning in punches.

'Don't turtle up!' shouts Bert. 'Keep your eyes on his chest.'

I look up just in time to see my opponent pivot at the hips and launch a big right cross through the gap between my gloves. *Game over*, I think to myself, and sure enough the next thing I know I'm lying on the canvas and Bert is counting to ten. In my mind I'm right back in the Tombs, lying on those chessboard tiles in the holding cell, surrounded by the crushed remains of Carmen's confetti chess set.

'Five, six, seven,' Bert counts. 'Come on, girl, get up.'

I press my knuckles to the floor, heave myself to my feet and raise my gloves to my face. Joshua smiles apologetically at me and moves forward, ready to start teeing off on my head again, but Bert puts out a hand to stop him.

'That's enough,' he says to Joshua, and then to me, 'Well done, girl.'

I shake my head groggily. 'Well done for what?'

'For getting up,' says Bert, gently unlacing my gloves. 'You never know what's inside a fighter until they're flat out on the canvas.'

I link my hands to give Teddy a leg up, then hop up onto the wall beside him. There we sit, swinging our legs, gazing at The House.

'Where are we?' asks Teddy.

'Number twenty-three West Tenth Street,' I say. 'Better known as The Marshall Club. Why do you think I've brought you here?'

'Bobby Fischer,' yawns Teddy. 'Game of the Century, right?'

'Geez, Teddy, how d'you get to hear about the Game of the Century?'

'My dad is always going on about it,' says Teddy. 'He says if I work hard I could be the next Bobby Fischer.'

'Believe me, you don't want to be the next Bobby Fischer. And no, I didn't bring you here to talk about Bobby. I brought you here to talk about the guy whose name is on the door.'

'Marshall?'

'You got it. Great player, Frank Marshall. US champion for twenty-seven years. In one tournament game he played a move so wonderful that the spectators showered the board with gold pieces.'

'Wow.' Teddy is impressed. 'Was he better than Capa?'

'No, the Cuban Chess Machine was in a league of his own. But Marshall did beat him a couple of times, including one time with the black pieces. Beating Capa with Black, Teddy, that was rare as rabbit horns.'

'Or horsefeathers,' giggles Teddy.

'You want to know what Marshall was best at? Swindling.'

'He was a con man?'

'Not exactly. In chess a swindle is a comeback. There's nothing bad or dishonest about it. It's when you're in the middle of a game and you're losing bad but you manage to find a way to claw yourself back into contention, maybe even win. Perhaps your remaining pieces can launch some sort of mating attack, or you can complicate the position so much that your opponent makes a blunder, or you find a way to force a stalemate.'

Teddy's face brightens. 'I did that to my dad once. He was killing me so bad he started singing "We are the Champions" and drumming on the table. Game ended up a stalemate.'

'Well then, that proves it. Resigning is for wimps, Teddy. Take a leaf from Frank Marshall's book. Dig deep. Find a way back. You've got your School Cup coming up next month and if I hear that you've resigned in any of your games, I'm going to come to your school with that onyx chessboard of yours and I'm going to beat you over the head with it.'

Teddy bursts out laughing. 'You'll have to catch me first,' he says, hopping off the wall and sprinting up the street.

MY PROBLEM

Bert says that sparring gets easier the more you do it. I think he's wrong. I think if anything it gets harder, because you know how much pain is about to come your way.

Unless you have tried sparring you can't understand how exhausting it is. A minute into each session I just want to sit down and get my energy back, but instead I have to keep moving, keep punching, keep thinking of ways to get past my opponent's guard, keep failing. I spar with a different partner every week, and every week I take a beating.

Stop letting them hit you with free jabs, Bert is always scolding me. *Not on the forehead, not on the chin, not anywhere, you got that? If they can tag you with a jab they can tag you with other shots. Keep your feet moving. Keep your head bobbing. Keep blocking shots with that right glove of yours. If you can stop the jab, they're going to get frustrated and start making mistakes.*

It hurts being punched, even with the headgear and the bigass gloves. Tip of the nose, that's the worst of all. Stings like hell and brings tears to your eyes.

After one sparring session I jump down off the apron and there in front of me is Sydney Campbell.

'Well done,' she says, handing me my towel. 'I can't believe you're still standing after all the heat that guy was laying on you.'

I wrap the towel around my shoulders and sit down heavily on a bench.

Sydney sits down next to me. 'I'd give you some advice,' she says, 'but I don't want us to argue again.'

'Try me.'

'Okay, here goes.' She lowers her voice almost to a whisper. 'You're strong and you've got good movement. But your anger is killing you. As soon as you got tagged on the nose there, you flared up like a Catherine Wheel and started lashing out all over the place. A clear head, Leah, that's what you need if you want to succeed in this game. You gotta control your emotions.'

I can think of several clever retorts, real zingers all of them. So what comes out of my mouth next is as surprising to me as it is to Sydney Campbell.

'Okay,' I say. 'I'll mention it to my therapist next time I see her.'

'How are you feeling today?' asks Daphne.

'Angry,' I say. 'I'm always angry, even when I'm not, if that makes any sense.'

Daphne nods and does her pained smile. It's one of the tools of her trade, that pained smile. I'll bet she practices it in front of the mirror each morning to get the pain-sympathy ratio just so.

She hands me a piece of paper and tells me to make a list of who I'm angry at and why. That's easy. I scribble my list in ten seconds flat and Daphne makes an elaborate show of not looking at what I'm writing.

1. The doctor (for dropping gallstones into Dad's bile duct)
2. Dad (for abandoning me)
3. Mom (for still being alive)
4. Everyone at the funeral (for saying and doing dumb stuff)
5. The rest of the world (for carrying on as if nothing happened)
6. Myself (for going to Rhode Island)
7. God (for making me *me*)

'Well done,' beams Daphne when I'm done. 'Acknowledging your anger is half the battle. And you know what, Leah? It's okay to feel angry. No seventeen-year-old should have to cope with what you've gone through.'

'Thank you, Daphne,' I whisper, and she rewards me with another pained smile.

I look up at the far corner of the room, but my seven-legged friend is no longer there. I guess he moved on.

CRUEL FAIR

On my way out of Daphne's office, I get a message from Kit. He wants to meet me at the fountain in Washington Square Park.

When I arrive, he's sitting on the stone steps staring at the fountain. As soon as he sees me he jumps to his feet.

'Haven't seen you in aeons!' he cries. 'Not since the Golden Compass turn'd through vast profundity obscure. Not since the birth of Nature from the unapparent Deep. Not since the Elemental Air diffused to utmost convex of the Earth.'

'Yeah. I've been busy. Shush now.'

I sit beside him on the cold stone step. He looks at me accusingly. 'You still on that dumb adrenalin trip of yours?'

'If you mean, am I still boxing, then yes. Did some more sparring today, as a matter of fact.'

'How was it?'

'Got my ass handed to me. All the stuff I'd practiced on the bag went right out of the window when I started getting hit in the head.'

Kit looks horrified. 'You show me who hit you in the head,' he declares, 'and I'll—'

'You'll what?'

'I'll censure them harshly in iambic pentameters.'

I laugh and elbow him in the ribs. I feel bad for having gone so long without seeing Kit, and now that I'm with him I'm glad of his company. I can be myself with Kit, and there's not many people I can say that about.

As I gaze into the water at my feet I see a sudden flash of red against the gray marble of the fountain base. There's something down there. I reach down and fish it out.

'Look, Kit. It's some sort of document pouch.'

'Wow,' says Kit. 'I wonder what's inside.'

I yank the plastic zipper and pull out a single sheet of paper, a sodden sheet which disintegrates wetly in my hand.

As I flick it off my fingers in disgust, Kit groans and clutches his forehead. 'That wasn't supposed to happen,' he says. 'The woman in the store assured me those pouches are water resistant.'

'What do you mean? What was that thing?'

'Nothing. A gift for you, that's all. A Mikhail Tal score sheet from the 1990 New York Open.'

'Handwritten by Tal?'

'Yes.'

'Signed?'

'Yes.'

'And you put it in the fountain?'

'Yes.' He stares miserably into the water. 'It was supposed to be romantic.'

'Romantic!' I get to my feet and shrug my gym bag onto my back. 'Kit, I'm flattered, but you need to stop buying me expensive stuff. I'm not your girlfriend.'

Kit looks at me. 'Maybe you should be.'

'Maybe I shouldn't.'

'Is it because my eyes are wonky?'

'No.'

'Yes, it is,' Kit mutters. 'You said so on your blog.'

Before I can stop him, he leaps to his feet and splashes forward into the fountain. He shivers underneath it, drenched from head to foot.

People are pointing and laughing, but that doesn't faze Kit. He raises his arms aloft and dances mournfully under the curtain of falling water. Then, just when I think he's reached peak weirdness, he starts to sing at the top of his voice:

'*So oft as I her beauty do behold, and therewith do her cruelty compare, I marvel of what substance was the mold, which made her all at once so cruel-fair!*'

My brain is screaming at me to just melt away into the crowd, but I instead I stay right where I am, yelling at Kit to come out of the fountain and talk to me. At long last he wades to the edge and climbs out, pale and shivering.

'Listen, you bozo.' I drape my coat around his shoulders. 'You remember what I said about the flesh-eating eagle? Well, it's still peckin' away. And I like you, I really do, but the last thing I need right now is a boyfriend.'

'Oh.'

'I could really use a friend, though—' My voice falters. 'A normal friend, you know? Someone to hang out with. Someone who's got my back. Someone who'll forgive me when I behave like a titan with a sore liver. I don't know, maybe I shouldn't even be asking this. It's not fair on you.'

Kit fiddles with the edge of the plastic document pouch. 'She told me this thing was waterproof,' he mutters. 'I'm going to get a refund.'

'You do that.'

We sit in silence, staring at that pouch like it contains the answer to every question we've ever asked ourselves.

'It's fine,' Kit says at last. 'I can be that person. A normal friend.'

'Can you?'

'Sure.' He pulls my coat tight around his body. 'And hey, I'll save a fortune on chess memorabilia.'

MIND GAME

Turns out Bert is right. Sparring does get easier the more you do it. Your stance, your guard, your movement, it all becomes instinctive and then one day you get in the ring with a sparring partner and you find yourself with time to think. You start to notice what your opponent is doing. You start to learn their preferences. You start to read them like you would read a chess opponent. You realize where you can hurt them.

I'm in the ring one afternoon, sparring with Joshua and eating leather as usual, when I notice that he always blocks my jab the same way, turning to his left and parrying with his right hand. So next time I get within range I try something new. I feint a jab and at the last moment turn it into a left hook. My gloved fist sneaks around Joshua's guard and clobbers his right ear, *whump!* As the delicious shock wave travels down my arm, my heart leaps in my chest.

I got him.

Joshua covers up and pivots to one side. I feint the jab, he moves his right hand over his ear and I go straight up the middle, tagging him on the cheek, *crack!*

'Attagirl!' cries Bert, delighted.

Some of the tension has gone from my body. I feel lighter, faster and more powerful. I slip my head to one side, bend my knees and throw a low jab which glances off Joshua's chest. I step back as if to move out of range, he goes to follow me and *pop!* I land a jab right on the end of his nose.

'It's landing,' cries Bert. 'Your jab is landing!'

In a sunburst of clarity I realize that boxing is just like blitz chess, a garden of forking paths. If you do that, I'll do this, and if you go there, I'll go here, and if you do that, I'll do THIS and I'll beat you, fish, because I'm stronger than you, ha!

Boxing is chess and chess is boxing. You learn the techniques, you put in the hours and then you step into the ring and it's like sitting down at a table in Washington Square Park. It's a mind game, pure and simple.

Flushed with success, I stand in the corner of the gym punching a body bag hard and fast. The bag is shuddering all over like it's having a seizure, just the way it should.

'Take that,' I hiss. 'And that, and that.'

'And you take THIS,' retorts the bag in a gruff Cookie Monster voice. It swings toward me and hits me hard in the chest, knocking me backward.

Peeking under the bag I glimpse a pair of well-muscled legs and blue high tops. I spring forward and throw a wide looping left hook around the back of the bag.

'Oof!' says the voice.

'Travis!' I feign surprise. 'Is that you?'

'I was just passing.' The bag rises up and away from me, groaning on its chain. 'You know how you said you don't dance?'

'Yes.'

'You might want to start now.'

I bob left and right, trying to anticipate the downward swing of the bag. Here it comes, accelerating toward me. I dive left, twist my body to dodge the swing, then grab it on the rebound and push the bag hard in Travis's direction. He backs away too slow and the bag thuds into his chest.

He's on the ground, winded. I stand over him, knocking my gloves together. 'Get up,' I tell him.

Travis gets up and we circle each other warily at range.

'Impressive reactions,' he says. 'Obi Wan has taught you well.'

'You like *Star Wars*?'

'Sure,' says Travis. 'Doesn't everyone?'

'You'd be surprised.'

I advance toward him, probing with my jab, backing him up into the corner of the gym. As soon as his back touches the wall, I unleash the combo I've been practicing at home these last few nights. Jab, right uppercut, left hook, straight right. The first three punches glance off his hands and forearms but the straight right cuts through his guard. He falls forward and we clinch.

'Thanks for the lessons,' I whisper. 'You've been really useful to me.'

'Useful? Is that what you look for in a guy?'

'Yes.' I spin out of the clinch. 'That and a good grasp of the Lucena position.'

'Never heard of it.'

'It's a thing in rook pawn endgames, but it's way beyond your skill level. When your rating hits two thousand, I'll show you Lucena.'

'That could be years away!'

I put my gloves into my kit bag and head for the exit.

'I said, that could be years away!' he shouts after me.

I hoik the bag onto my shoulder and trot up the stairs into the fresh afternoon air.

PART THREE: ENDGAME

Every pawn is a potential queen

James Mason (1849–1905)

Wow. I can't believe how much time has gone by since I last wrote an update.

I've always liked writing, and it's good having a record of all the dumb stuff that happens to me, but my problem now is time. I got so busy with chess and boxing and coaching and therapy, I found I couldn't do it all AND write about it.

Why start writing again now? Because I'm entering my endgame, that's why. Leah 'Park Girl' Baxter just got herself a bout at the Elephant Club.

The endgame, that's the thing! It's the fight at the end of the tunnel. It's the ultimate challenge: put up or shut up.

I often think about my first meeting with Charles Croft, when he asked me to teach Teddy some nifty openings that would fox the older kids. Well, here we are TWO YEARS later and I still haven't taught Teddy any 'nifty openings', not even Blackmar-Diemer. And here's why. Unless you have a deep understanding of chess, nifty openings aren't worth diddly squat. You think some half-baked gambit you found on YouTube is going to revolutionize your chess? It won't. It's more likely to stick a knife in your back and bury you on the beach with the tide coming in.

Quit obsessing about openings, that's what I tell my students. It's the endgame where the real rewards lie. It's the endgame where the power and subtlety of each piece is revealed in its purest form, and where patient, accurate play can transform the stalest of draws into the sweetest of victories.

The Cuban Chess Machine José Raúl Capablanca was the greatest endgame player the world has ever seen. His endgame was even better than Tal's, and that's saying something. For two years Teddy and I have been playing through Capa's endgames, discussing them move by move. This does more for Teddy's chess than any number of books on opening strategy. He has learnt how to transform his endgame king from a timorous cowering beastie into a stout-hearted warrior. He has learnt to play on both wings so that his opponent's troops are stretched to breaking point. He has learnt to time his pawn breaks to perfection and he has even ventured into the terrifying labyrinth of the double rook endgame, where grown men weep and gnash their teeth under the mental strain.

The endgame, that's the thing. It's where all roads lead.

BILLBOARD

'Rooks on the seventh rank are big fat hogs, Teddy. They eat everything in sight. If you can get both your rooks to the seventh rank, your opponent's defensive line becomes one long feeding trough.'

We are sitting in the Crofts' dining room, studying Capablanca's Round 8 game from the New York tournament of 1918. Teddy reads the moves off his phone and replays them on the plastic board in front of us. When he arrives at White's resignation, he gives the king a good hard flick, sending it skidding across the mahogany table top and onto the floor.

These days I have seven chess students, all different ages, but Teddy is still my favorite. Since I started teaching him, he has added four hundred points to his rating and has lifted the School Cup two years in a row. Later this month his father is taking him to Richmond to compete in the Under-ten Nationals. I think he has a chance of winning.

Teddy leans back in his chair and grins at me. 'My sister said she saw you on a billboard this afternoon,' he says.

'Times Square?' I joke.

'No, Hell's Kitchen. She said there were three other people in the picture too, and one of them was some kind of monster with a skull for a face. Van was crying when she told me – that's how scared she was.'

'Poor Van. They shouldn't put scary pictures on the street where kids can see them. The woman with the skull tattoos is Zelda Haas, Women's Chessboxing Champion of the World. She's at the Elephant Club tomorrow night, taking on my friend Sydney Campbell. It's going to be epic.'

'You're fighting the winner?'

'No chance. I'm fighting before the main event, to get everyone in the mood. I'm up against some hotshot French woman called Odette Segal. Her nickname is *La Dangereuse*.'

'The Dangerous One,' translates Teddy. 'She gonna kick your butt.'

'Yeah?' I jump to my feet. 'Not before I kick yours.'

I chase Teddy around and around the mahogany table. He squeals in pretend fright and pushes chairs into my path to slow me down. On his third lap of the table he steps on the slain white king and goes flying through the air like Accident Amy skidding on a banana skin.

The door opens and Mary Croft comes into the room holding a tray. 'Milk and cookies for the grandmasters!' she announces, but when she sees her son lying on his back with his legs in the air her smile fades. 'Theodore, darling, are you all right?'

'Slipped on a chess piece,' he mutters, looking daggers at the offending king.

'Is that so?' says Mrs Croft, looking daggers at me.

The night before my big fight, I make pizza for me and Mom. Pizza is good for carb-loading, and also because I can pretend that the dough is Odette Segal. I set to work on it with unbridled aggression, jabbing and pummeling it into submission.

'Hey, Leah!' Mum pokes her head around the door. 'Will the pizza be long?'

'No, Mama!' I cry out in what I imagine to be an Italian accent. 'It will be round!'

It's an old joke but we cackle like hyenas all the same. Mom pours herself a large glass of red wine and plonks herself down at the kitchen table.

'You want some, Leah?' She waves the bottle airily.

'No, Mama.' (I like this accent, I think I'll keep it up all night.) 'Tomorrow is my big fight, remember?'

Of course she remembers. She frowns and takes a big slug of wine.

I make the passata, grate the mozzarella, then return to the dough, stretching and twirling it with ever more extravagant gestures and practicing my footwork around the table. *Step, drag, forward, back, step, drag, forward, back.* The dough is soft and springy, whirling on my floury fingertips.

'Will there be a doctor on hand?' Mom asks suddenly.

'*Mama Mia!*' I cry. 'What are you saying about my pizza? I have never been so insulted in all my living days! I tell you, Mama, my pizza is the best pizza in all of—'

'Leah.' Mom reaches out and puts a hand on my arm. 'Will there be a doctor on hand?'

'Yes, Mom.' I lay down the dough. 'The safety of the fighters is paramount. There's a ringside physician just outside the ropes, and she has complete power to suspend or terminate the fight at any time.'

FIGHT NIGHT

'*Ladies and gentlemen, welcome to New York's premier chessboxing venue, the Elephant Club. This is the hottest ticket in town, and boy are you in for a treat tonight. The spectacle that awaits you is the ultimate in hybrid sport, a dazzling celebration of the depth and breadth of human endeavor. This is where knight . . . meets fight! Where pawn . . . meets brawn! Mate the king . . . or win in the ring! Tonight we are serving up for your delectation a truly sensational event involving two of the greatest – no, THE two greatest – female chessboxers of all time, competing in an official WCBO title challenge. Are you excited for this, ladies and gentlemen?*'

A rafterbusting cheer rises from the throng. Marcus Crockett lifts his arms in the air and milks the applause as long as he can. I wait in the wings, shifting my weight from foot to foot, trying in vain to calm my galloping heartbeat. Got my mouth guard in my pocket, got my high tops on my feet. Here it comes, the moment I've been preparing for these last two years.

'Before we serve up the main course, allow us to present you with a mouth-watering hors d'oeuvre, a curtain-raiser so electrifying you'll feel the buzz in every neurone. Ladies and gentlemen, I'm delighted to introduce two top-notch fighters bursting with personality and skill. One is a veteran of the European chessboxing scene. The other is a young home-grown talent. I gotta tell you, folks, I have been pumped up for this bout ever since it was scheduled, and I'm so excited I can hardly speak.'

A colossal subwoofer next to me booms out its rumbles of anticipation. I crouch down beside it and pull the curtain aside to peek at the crowd. Strobing spotlights illuminate a sea of eager upturned faces. Travis stands in the front row. He is hugging his shoulders and his lips are a thin hard line.

Travis has done well these last two years. He headlined an Elephant Club fight card against Pietro 'The Skewer' Scaramucci, stopping him in the fifth round with a cheeky back rank mate. He knocked out the Brazilian fighter Sambisto 'Hamfisto' Correa ten seconds into their first boxing round, and last fall in Montreal he fought the great Albanian chessboxer Kreshnik Paloka. Drew the chess game and lost narrowly on boxing countback. Travis was devastated but his performance won him the Best Newcomer award from the World Chessboxing Association. Oh, and thanks to me his FIDE rating is pushing 1930. Not bad for a jock.

A tap on my shoulder makes me start. I look up to see a pockmarked face with an angry scar above and below the right eye and a bulge at the top of the nose where it reset badly after a break. This is *La Dangereuse*, just as ugly in real life as on her YouTube channel.

'When this fight is over,' she says with a thick French accent, 'you too will be unable to speak.'

'Only because I'll be too busy laughing,' I say.

'*Fighting out of the blue corner, official weight 132 pounds, she gives me the crêpes, she drives me in-Seine, she punched me, Ei-fel. All the way from belle Paris, please give it up for the legend of legerdemain, Odette "La Dangereuse" Segal!*'

A volley of French gangster rap blasts from the speakers. Cheers and whistles ring out across the club. Segal pushes past me and strides out along the walkway toward the ring. It's not real, that scar of hers. It's lipstick. Like her chessboard boxing gloves, it's a reference to *Froid Equateur*, the French graphic novel which first made chessboxing a thing.

'Fighting out of the red corner, official weight 127 pounds, a chessboxing débutante whose tender age is the only tender thing about her. Please give it up for Made in Manhattan, International Master, YouTube sensation, Supreme Ruler of the Land of Sass, Leah "Park Girl" Baxter!'

I step out into the spotlight and walk to the ring, trying to look like someone who belongs in a boxing club and isn't scared out of her wits. I duck down to climb through the ropes, but my opponent comes right over and blocks the gap so I can't get through. I'm bent over double with my head pressing against her abs.

Don't get mad, I tell myself. *Let her have her dumb intimidation tactics. Stay cool. Stay focussed.*

I push her out of my way and straighten up.

'Tu es tellement petite que ta tête pue des pieds,' she sneers. 'You're so small, your head stinks of feet.'

'Yeah?' I say. 'You're so big you're gonna make an impact crater the size of Central Park when I knock . . . you . . . out.'

I punctuate the last three words with three air jabs toward her face. The crowd whoops and jeers. They're juiced up for this, and so am I.

I take off my gloves, sit down at the board and put on my headphones. La Dangereuse is still trash talking but I can't hear a word she is saying. I just sit there ignoring her and adjusting my white pieces on their squares. This board is *my* domain. Ain't nobody gonna boss me here.

We shake hands and the referee starts the clock.

I open pawn e4 and she replies straightaway with d5. It's that most irritating of all chess openings, the Scandinavian Defense. I could easily transpose into a Blackmar-Diemer Gambit with pawn d4, but Segal has probably been studying my past games and preparing a refutation. Besides, I've kind of fallen out of love with Blackmar-Diemer these last two years. That GM Hammett quote comparing BDG to ritual suicide? He might have had a point.

I take the pawn on d5. Segal retakes with her queen. I attack with my knight and immediately she slides her queen across to a5. She has chosen by far the most aggressive line of the Scandinavian, the line that says *I'm coming for you, punk.*

I'm toying with the idea of pawn b4 but that's an ultrasharp gambit and I'm worried I might lose my way when I start getting punched in the head. *Keep it simple*, I tell myself. *Keep developing pieces. Give her just enough rope to hang herself.*

I push my d pawn. She pushes her c pawn. I develop my kingside knight. She brings out her queenside bishop. I consider pawn h3 but there's no hurry to do that yet. What was it Coach used to say? *The only time you should hurry is when you're robbing a bank.*

I slide a bishop to f4. It's hardly a ground-breaking move, but Segal does not respond to it. Just sits there staring at the board for minute after minute, twirling her braids around a thick finger. I know what she's doing and I can't say I blame her. She doesn't want to play on just yet.

She wants to hit me in the head and then play on.

ROUND 2

The card girl parades around the ring with her fake tan and her Round 2 card. Odette Segal prances behind her, waving and flexing and mugging for the crowd. A team of deft stagehands carry away the board, clocks, chairs and table. Marcus Crockett is gabbling into the mic, listing the highlights of Segal's former kickboxing career. I feel sick.

Dad, I whisper. *Help me.*

I slug two mouthfuls of water, squirt some on my brow and pull on my boxing gloves. The ref ducks between the ropes, pristine in his white Oxford shirt, black slacks, black leather shoes and black bow tie. He signals for us to come together and I approach the Frenchwoman cautiously, my heart hammering in my chest.

Keep moving, I remind myself. *Bob and weave and work the angles. Get your jab landing, then go for the big shots.* The bell rings and we come together, circling and feinting. Segal taps her gloves together and *yop!* she hits me on the cheek.

I stumble backward out of range. I hadn't even realized I *was* in range. She hit me from about four feet away with that long left arm of hers.

Yop! she tags me again and I'm on the back foot and now she's coming at me hard and combo after combo is glancing off my gloves. I'm ducking and bobbing and trying to stand my ground and keep my guard up but the game plan has gone right out of my head and instead there's nothing but the white-hot rush of fear. The ropes are taut against my back and Segal is in my face snorting and punching like a freak. With nowhere to go I loop my arms around her and hug her tight to stop the onslaught. She smells of soap and sweat.

Breathe. Breathe. My forehead is resting on Segal's shoulder blade and I'm sucking in oxygen and waiting for the referee to break us apart. Has he given the order yet? I can't hear him for the baying of the crowd. Segal's muscles flex, her left arm wriggles free and the next thing I know my legs are gone from under me and I'm on the canvas.

What just happened?

An uppercut to the liver, that's what happened, and my whole abdomen is on fire like I've been injected with a needleful of nitric acid. Travis is there in front of me. He puts his fingers to the corners of his mouth and draws a smile.

He's right. When you get snuffed real bad you need to smile, not because it didn't hurt but because you have to show your opponent that you are still confident. You have to show her that nothing she does is going to stop you.

I drag myself to my feet and smile like a paper cut. But I can't stand up straight and the ref is looking at me quizzically. *Do you want to go on?*

I raise my gloves and nod.

Segal smirks and swaggers toward me, shoulders high and choppy, elbows out to the sides, gloves behind her back to taunt me.

'*Viens!*' she calls to me. '*Viens ici, ma petite!*'

Her right hand moves up to her face but her left still dangles by her side. I feint a jab. She bobs and pivots, goading me to commit to a big punch. I'm not playing that game. I'll keep my straight rights warm for her and I'll serve them up when I'm good and ready.

La Dangereuse taps her gloves together and surges forward, her fist sneaking underneath my guard right into my gut. I watch the skin shiver across my midriff and then comes the pain, hard and white like the floodlight on the ring, and once again I'm backing away, jabbing for dear life, wheezing and gasping and longing for the bell.

There it is at last, clear and sweet, a cow-bell in the mountains.

Segal struts to the ropes, cups a hand around her ear and grins at the crowd like a jackass eating cactus. She's taunting them for having gone so quiet, and it's true, they have. Their home-grown golden girl is getting mashed.

I pull off my gloves and gulp water from my bottle. A team of stagehands bounds into the ring and sets up the chess table. Marcus Crockett gabbles into the mic, recounting the horror of the boxing round in gory detail.

Rout. Drubbing. Mismatched. Doomed. Good colorful words, but he's wrong about doomed, for in the pain and panic of that last exchange, I noticed something about Segal. She always taps her gloves together just before she launches an attack.

It's her tell.

ROUND 3

My head is pounding as I take my place at the chess table. 'Hey, Segal,' I pant. 'Do you speak German?'

'No.'

'You're welcome.'

By the time my meaning dawns on her I've got my headphones on and can't hear a word of her reply. I center my pieces on their squares and suck air deep into my lungs. This is the hardest thing about chessboxing: sitting down to calculate when your body is flooded with adrenalin. To prepare for this moment, I've been playing 'stair chess' every morning: blitz games against Rybka interspersed with lung-searing sprints to the top of our apartment block and back.

It's Segal's turn to move. She plays e6. I play h3. Bishop takes knight. *Breathe.*

Queen takes bishop. *Breathe.* I've weathered the storm of those *Cold Equator* boxing gloves and now I'm back where I belong on solid maple and rosewood. Nothing about this position fazes me. It's classic Scandinavian.

Bishop b4. *Breathe.* Bishop e2. *Breathe.* Knight d7. That's odd. I was expecting the other knight to come out. Surely she can't be intending to castle on her weakened queenside? What would be the point? Pressure on d4? Pawn storm on the kingside?

I push a pawn to a3, where it eyes her dark-squared bishop. Segal hunches forward and rubs the bulge on the bridge of her nose. If she wants to, she can force another bishop-knight exchange, but that doesn't worry me. I would happily play an endgame with two bishops against two knights, providing I have enough time left on the clock to keep a lookout for forks.

Segal takes hold of her king as if to castle, then lets it go like it's electrified and goes to grab her bishop instead. The referee stops her. Touch-move has been a basic rule of chess for five hundred years. I know it. Segal knows it. Even the patzers in the crowd know it. The piece you touched first is the one you have to move.

My opponent heaves a deep sigh and castles long. The gasp, the sigh, it's all an elaborate con, of course, a pathetic pantomime to make me believe she's blundered. She is desperate for me to snap up her bishop with my pawn. If I fall into the trap, her queen swoops down the open 'a' file and captures my rook, winning the exchange and probably the game.

What does she imagine? That I've been studying at the Tom Foolery School of Chessic Mindlessness? That I'm going to leap high in the air like Archimedes and rush to gobble up the poisoned bishop? That I'll leap into a one-ply patzer trap on the strength of her lame-ass theatrics?

Does she not realize who she's playing?

Assuming I ignore the bait, what then? Castle on opposite sides, exchange on c3, slap a rook on the open b file and launch an attack? That's playable. With the enemy king on c8 my dark-squared bishop is a monster, peering right along the diagonal into the depths of her fortress. I gaze at the probing bishop and a lightning bolt flashes across my brain.

If only I could lure her queen away from the 'a' file . . .

I lean forward and lace my fingers across my forehead. My surroundings disappear and I am all alone in a garden of forking paths. It is unexpectedly beautiful, this garden. All the main paths are pleasing to the eye and one in particular is utterly sublime.

ROUND 4

Somebody stops the clocks, lifts up the chessboard and bears it away. I raise my head from my hands and stand up unsteadily in the harsh white light. Segal has her gloves on already. She is bouncing on the balls of her feet, splitting the air with savage punches.

I blink hard and cast around for my gloves and mouthpiece. Wrenched out of my intricate calculations I feel groggy and disorientated, like I've just woken up from a deep sleep. *Come on*, I tell myself. *Time to fight. Let's go.*

The bell sounds. Segal and I snap together and raise our guards, circling each other at the limit of our range.

Wait for the tell. Wait for the tell. There. Segal taps her gloves together and steps in behind a jab.

This time I'm ready for her. I roll my shoulder and explode straight into the counter punch. *Crack*, I tag her hard on the

247

forehead. Segal winces and sucks in her breath but she recovers real fast and bounces back with a huge overhand right that misses my head by a whisker. I throw an uppercut. She sees it coming and rolls with it, dissipating its power.

I step forward inside her guard and we set about each other with a thousand cruel shots. Her height advantage and her incredible reach are no longer advantages because we're nose to nose and toe to toe in a blistering scrap for survival. It's not pretty, this slugfest, but the crowd are roaring their approval. *Don't step back*, I tell myself. *You've got her rocked. Stay right where you are and slug it out.*

I'm so close to Segal that I feel rather than see her shots coming at me. She winds up a left hook, I duck underneath. She throws an uppercut, I clam up tight. She bends her knees, desperate to make herself small, but I'm the smaller, tighter package, a born inside fighter, a whirlwind of short crisp lefts and snappy rights. I'm swinging my hips to generate power, searching for the angle that will put her raggedy ass to sleep.

At long last my opponent slumps forward exhausted and we embrace like lovers. Her arms are around my shoulders. My right arm hovers warily over my liver, protecting it from harm.

'Break!' shouts the ref, and with one explosive movement *La Dangereuse* spins out of the clinch and snuffs me on the chin.

We're back at the chessboard. Adrenalin trickles away and a tide of exquisite pain floods in. I narrow my eyes and try to focus, but the board is incoherent. I can't even remember the name of the opening that gave rise to this position. Something to do with candy?

A woman in a white coat stands just outside the ring, leaning on a rope. She watches me closely, frowning. I scowl back at her. Too many people staring at me. Too many people expecting me to perform wonders like some dumbass street magician.

The button on my clock is in the up position. Her move or mine? I stare down at the board. I remember now. I was going to make a capture.

Five hundred years ago they had different names for each pawn, depending on which piece it protects. Gambler, Guard, Innkeeper, Blacksmith, Moneychanger, Doctor . . .

Doctor! The woman in the white coat is the ringside doctor. And the rook's pawn on the far left of the board, the one I'm looking at right now, he's the Gambler.

My wrapped fingers rise painfully from the table top and move toward the pawn. *Extensor muscles, fire!* My hand opens. *Flexor muscles, fire!* I grasp the Gambler's head between my fingertips.

I glance at the man with the curly graying hair and the microphone. He is shaking his head. He looks appalled. Perhaps he left the iron on at home.

Extensor muscles, fire! Flexor muscles, fire!

I capture the bishop and the scarred face across the board from me cracks into a horrible grin. Already her queen is on the move, charging toward me along its checkered corridor. *Bam*, she takes my rook and slaps the button on her clock.

My king is in check, so I nudge him forward out of the firing line, and *yop!* Segal sweeps her queen across the board to take my other rook. I remember her nickname now. *The Dangerous One.* Although I can't hear anything, the shape of her mouth suggests that she is laughing.

No matter. My mouth is laugh-shaped too. Why should it be otherwise? A million years ago in another lifetime I visualized this path, and sure, it's kind of funny. It's good that we can laugh together as we walk it.

I pick up my queen and bump off an Innkeeper on my opponent's side of the board. *Check.* The Dangerous One grabs a Guard and retakes straightaway, leering and smirking all over her face. She is a queen and two rooks up, enough to delight even the greediest of materialists. But on this narrow, beautiful path, material gains are irrelevant. *What profits a woman if she gains the whole world and loses her own soul?*

I pick up my light-squared bishop and slide it up the board as far as it will go.

Bishop to a6.

Checkmate.

My head slumps down onto my forearm. The woman in the white coat ducks between the ropes and hurries toward me. She straightens my legs, places my arms across my chest, removes my mouthpiece and runs her hands gently down the back of my neck.

Once upon a time there was an English landscape artist called Samuel Standidge Boden. Like all Victorian landscape artists, he painted babbling rivers, dozing sheep, rose-clad cottages and rose-cheeked kids. He also loved playing chess.

'Leah, I am going to ask you a few questions. Please listen carefully and give your best effort. What is your full name? Where are we? How many fingers am I holding up?'

In 1853 Samuel Standidge Boden played an old master visiting from Germany. He checkmated the master with two criss-crossing bishops, a simple and elegant mating pattern which became known as Boden's mate. A pattern worthy of a true artist. To see a Boden's mate in tournament play is as rare and precious as finding an original Boden watercolor in a backstreet flea market.

'Look at me, Leah. Who is the President of the United States of America? Who is the current World Chess Champion? How many legs does an insect have?'

I blink hard and look up at my questioner. 'Six,' I tell her. 'The Lepidopteran larva looks like it has sixteen legs, but only six of them are actual legs. The others are stumpy pro-legs. Not real legs at all.'

'I didn't know that,' laughs the doctor. 'Off you go. Enjoy your moment.'

Marcus Crockett grabs my hand and thrusts it into the air. Pyrotechnics explode around the stage. Spectators cheer and clench their fists. Down in the pit Travis whips off his T-shirt and bellows like a bare-chested thunder orc.

'Your winner, ladies and gentlemen. Leah "Park Girl" Baxter!'

Can you see me, Dad? Are you proud of me? This one is for you.

BACKSTAGE

The corridor backstage at the Elephant Club is like something out of an *Alien* movie – all metal piping and flickering ceiling lights. On my way back to my dressing room I run into Syd Campbell swishing along in a scarlet gown, a picture of poise and determination. A stagehand limps behind her, two heavy-ass kit bags across his shoulders. That's what you get when you're US champion. A hobbit to carry your bags.

'I knew you'd do it!' yells Syd, grabbing my face between her wrapped hands. 'I listened to every second of Crockett's commentary in the dressing room. Boden's mate, you saucy bi-atch!'

'Guilty,' I laugh. 'Good luck in your own bout, Syd.'

Her expression hardens. 'I don't need luck. I just need Key and Peele here to do their stuff.'

I've warned her that nothing good can come of naming her fists, but Syd doesn't care what I think. Never has, never will.

The US women's chessboxing champion strides off toward the arena, her hobbit hobbling in her wake. I stand there in the corridor and watch them go.

Then I remember Mom.

Mom couldn't bear to come and watch the fight, so I promised to message her straight afterward. I grab my phone out of my kit bag and type quickly.

Mom, I won and I'm okay xx

I'm putting my phone back in the bag when suddenly a door flies open and a tall, hooded figure steps out into the corridor right in front of me.

The figure turns toward me and raises a scythe. The bulb in the panel above my head flares and flickers. I stare transfixed at the crescent blade, and then, beneath the cowl, I glimpse a row of long, bare tooth roots – the eternal, implacable smile of a skull.

Time stops.

I gaze into the face of Death and Death sneers back at me.

Don't look away, I tell myself.

I have seen her many times in pictures and in dreams, but never in real life. She's a work of art, this woman. Shadowy eye sockets. Hinged jaw. Hollow cheeks. Ridged temples. Jagged nasal bone. Must have taken many hours and more than one sitting.

At last, Haas turns away. She stalks off in the direction of the arena, her cowl and scythe still silhouetted in the flickering light.

ICE

I lower myself into my ice bath, open-mouthed and gasping with the shock of it. *Stay in, girl. Stay in the water. Stay in.* I concentrate on my breathing and work myself slowly into a pattern of long, deep breaths.

An ice bath after a big fight tightens your blood vessels and reduces the inflammation in your joints and muscles. Hurts like needles to a nerve but does a power of good.

Bathe, relax, I murmur. Kit once told me that Leah Baxter is an anagram of BATHE, RELAX, and now I can't help thinking of him when I take an ice bath. I wish he had come to the club to see me win.

Over on the bench my phone is pinging nonstop with Twitter mentions and press requests. Of course it is. Three minutes of vicious inside boxing followed by two rook sacs, a queen sac and Boden's mate? That thing will be pinging for weeks.

From the relay speaker in the corner of the locker room I can hear Marcus Crockett's breathless commentary. The headline fight between Syd and Haas is in full swing and it sounds like my friend is being trounced, both on the board and in the ring.

I feared as much. Key and Peele are no match for Death.

The discomfort of the ice bath has subsided a little so I let myself sink down until my head is under the water line and the ice blocks are bobbing above me.

Leah Baxter. Bathe, relax.

I hold my breath. My mind is sharp and clear. I comprehend with crystal clarity that winning a curtain-raiser will never be enough for me.

I've got to be World Champion.

I've got to get a fight with Zelda Haas.

At my weekly meeting with Daphne Piano, she claps her hand over her mouth and stares in horror at my two black eyes.

'All is well,' I tell her. 'It's just surface bruising.'

'Does it hurt?'

'Yes.'

'And this was from a boxing chess fight?'

'Chessboxing,' I correct her. 'Last Saturday night at the Elephant Club. Best night of my life, unless you count that night in Gibraltar when Elena Melnikova taught me how to break an apple in half with my bare hands.'

'Do you want to talk about Saturday night?' she asks.

'No, thank you. I'd rather talk about the usual. Grief and all.'

'All right.' Daphne pushes a plate of Oreos toward me. 'I was wondering, Leah, have you experienced any lifting lately?'

'Bench-pressed one-sixty last week.'

Daphne waves a hand as if to swat my joke out of the air. 'I know you don't like it when I talk about the stages of grief,' she says, 'but before you arrived this morning, I was reflecting on our two years together, and I was thinking that perhaps the fog might have lifted a little.'

'Maybe,' I say. I take an Oreo and twist the two halves gently back and forth until they come apart.

'Lifting does not mean instant happiness,' says Daphne. 'It's more about gradual acceptance. You wake up one day and you find yourself thinking about the future. Making plans. Slowly reconstructing your life.'

'Setting yourself goals?'

'Exactly!' She beams. 'I'm not saying that the grief goes away. I'm talking about a mysterious process whereby you grow to envelop the grief. You encompass it, if that makes any sense. There's a quotation in one of these books that puts it rather neatly.' She gets up and moves to her bookshelf.

While Daphne is hunting for her book, I lift the white half of the Oreo to my mouth and start to scrape off the filling with my teeth. I scrape and lick until both halves are clean and bare, then pop one half into each cheek, being careful not to break them.

'Aha! Here it is!' Daphne slips a paperback off the top shelf and turns to face me. I leer back at her, my cheeks bulging like a hamster.

Daphne puts the book down. She bends low over her desk, pretending to consult my client notes. 'Remind me, Leah,' she says. 'Are you nineteen or nine?'

There is a short silence and then we both burst out laughing at exactly the same moment. I have to clap my hand over my mouth so as not to spray cookie fragments everywhere.

'Sorry,' I say, when my mouth is empty enough to talk. 'I don't know what came over me. And I think I get what you're saying about growing to encompass the grief. It's like you're playing White in a complicated middlegame and a pesky black knight has gone and found itself an outpost on f4. It's a total monster and you can't see any way to dislodge it. You can resign right there and then, or you can find a way to, I don't know, work around it.'

Daphne nods and writes something down. 'Well put,' she says. 'Have another cookie.'

ACHILLES

Washington Square Park is pretty at any time of year, but in the fall it's incredible. The copper, rust and scarlet trees sway nonchalantly in the breeze, as though this sudden, mind-melding beauty of theirs were really nothing special.

I pull my scarf tighter around my neck and plunge my fists into my pockets. The park is busy today. Strollers stroll.

Joggers jog. Kids cavort in a jungle gym. An old man leans on a walking stick and watches a floppy-eared dog frolicking in a pile of crunchy leaves. A teenage girl in black jeans sits cross-legged on a bench, scribbling in a notebook, her hair falling in lank curtains on either side of the pen.

I glance at the chess tables as I pass. Deserted, save for two homeless guys playing checkers. The city's gambling laws were updated last year to include games of perfect information. When that happened, the Poisoned Pawns disbanded and went their separate ways. I still meet Kit two or three times a week to play chess in the park, but only for pleasure, never for cash.

I head on up to Holley Plaza, where the smell of cinnamon envelops me. Opposite the hot drinks wagon, a young man with wonky eyes sits quietly at a folding table, a piece of cardboard propped up in front of him. POEMS FOR PEANUTS reads the card.

'Kit!' I yell, hurrying toward him.

'Leah!' He jumps to his feet. We hug.

Kit graduated from high school back in June and is now studying English and American literature at NYU. He comes here every Saturday to run his POEMS FOR PEANUTS stall, just like he did before I met him.

'How's it going?' I ask.

'Same as always,' he grins. 'I've got a better view than any other desk worker in the city. Only problem is, hardly anyone seems to need poetry.'

'I need poetry,' I say.

I explain to Kit that I've decided to challenge Zelda Haas to a title bout. 'I've been watching her on YouTube,' I tell him. 'She's a great chess player, but I'm greater. Which means, all I have to do is hold my own in the boxing rounds. And all YOU have to do is to write me some battle rap for YouTube. Something that'll get under Zelda's skin and make her agree to face me.'

Kit sits back down at his table. 'I don't do battle rap,' he says. 'I'm more of a Coleridge man.'

'Then now's your chance to expand your repertoire. Come on, Kit, I need to challenge her in a way that will get her attention, or better still the attention of a big fight promoter. Write me some good bars and I'll do the rest.'

'I never knew ducks liked acorns,' says Kit, pointing at three ducks underneath an oak tree. The ducks are pecking at the pale brown nuts, crushing them in their bills.

'Hey! Don't change the subject.'

'I already told you, I'm not doing it.'

'Fine, don't do it.' I pick up an acorn and fling it at the ducks. 'But just supposing you did do it—'

'Leah!'

'Supposing you did do it, what sort of thing would you write?'

Kit sighs and runs a hand through his hair. It's down to his shoulders now. It suits him. 'I don't know,' he says. 'I guess you could start off with a eulogy, like you're fangirling her, then suddenly go cold and hard. Mock her. Needle her. Make her mad. Then, BAM, you come in with your main message: *I challenge you to a title bout.* That's the important bit, so make each word a hammer blow.'

'That's it? That's the end?'

'No, that's just taxi-ing up the runway. After that you take off and soar. You tell her what you're going to do to her, how you're going to take her apart, not just in the chess rounds but in the boxing too. You speed up your delivery, you start to move about a bit, you get cute with her. Champions usually take themselves way too seriously, so your job is to make her a laughing stock. Conjure some memorable images. Make her lie awake at night thinking about you. What's her mother tongue?'

'German.'

'Well then, sprinkle some German words in there. Use her heart language to really stick it to her. She won't forget that in a hurry!'

He's right, of course. He's always right about poetry. But ideas on their own aren't worth a plug nickel. I need words.

'Can you write it now?' I ask, trying to sound casual.

'Not now. Not any time.'

I take a bag of peanuts out of my coat pocket and plonk it down on the table between us. 'Poems for peanuts?'

Kit smiles. 'Nice try, but no.'

'Noodles?' I slap down a packet of picante beef Ramen.

Kit hoots with laughter. 'No!'

'Fine. Money, then.'

'I don't want your money.'

'I'll play chess with you.'

'You do that anyway.'

'I'll kiss you.'

'Don't talk cheap.'

'Then do it for the sake of our friendship.' I crouch down next to him. 'Please, Kit, do this one tiny thing and I'll never ask you to do anything else for me as long as I live.'

Kit looks at me for what seems like an age. Then he heaves a sigh and reaches for his pen.

'Okay,' he says. 'For friendship.'

An hour and a half later I leave Washington Square Park through the triumphal arch, a poem in my pocket and a flurry of golden leaves tumbling around me.

I guess the trees are entering their endgame too.

BERLIN

120 Leipziger Straße in Berlin is the international headquarters of the World Chessboxing Organization. I stand on a patch of grass across the road from the towering façade, glaring up at it with fire in my belly. Berlin is the epicenter of chessboxing on Planet Earth. It also happens to be the home town of Zelda Haas.

'You filming?' I ask Kit.

He nods. 'Whenever you're ready.'

I'm not really in Berlin. I'm in front of a green screen in a back room of the Elephant Club. The WCBO headquarters will be added in afterward by a guy called Graham.

I take a deep breath and step toward the camera, clenching my wrapped hands into fists. I've been practicing Kit's bars all weekend and I know them off by heart. Now I just need to deliver them right.

Confidence. Swagger. Breath control. Go.

'WCBO Ground Zero
Home of Zelda Haas, my hero
In the ring you're Miss Bombastic
On the board you're light fantastic
That's right, hon, I'm being sarcastic
Even your dumb scythe is plastic!'

Breathe. Breathe. My knees are trembling, but I don't break
eye contact, not for a second.

'Phantasmagoric, quick and cold
Alas, poor Yorick, your shtick got old
The Spandau freak show want you back
You clapped-out egomaniac
I'm here today to call you out
I challenge you to a title bout
I'll shove my glove right up your colon
Like Reshevsky, I fear NO ONE!'

Breathe. Breathe. I'm dancing in my high tops now, jabbing
my wrapped hands from side to side.

'I googled "champion Zelda Haas"
I swear I heard my laptop laugh
You think you're lit? You're standard edition
Skullduggery Schmidt from the Patzerdivision
I'm Mikhail Tal, you're Mickey Mouse
I'll put you in the Krankenhaus

And all will cry, "Beware Beware
The Sensenfrau's on gas and air!"
A Baxter backstep hook destroyed her
Let's get cooked on Schadenfreude!'

My right hand is down by my hip, flicking to and fro like I'm hurling ninja stars. I'm feeling the flow through my whole body and I'm feeling something else as well: molten rage, rising in my chest.

'Death be not proud, your chess is dull
In three rounds you'll be rendered null
You're old and slow, I'm fast and young
You've got two chances: Slim and None—
No, wait, I'm wrong, Slim cut and run
When you popped out to ink your tongue.'

I bulge my eyes like a warrior and stick my tongue out. Then I jump forward, right up close to the camera. I place my wrapped hands on either side of the lens and spit the last bars hard and clear.

'Guten Morgen, Sensenfrau
Have I got your attention now?
You choose the place, you choose the date
I'll prove you're an invertebrate
I'll reap your soul with Boden's mate
And keep your skull as a PAPERWEIGHT.'

As the last word leaves my mouth, the tension in my body erupts and I shove Kit away from me with terrifying force. He staggers and falls to the floor but somehow manages to steady the camera and point it up at me again.

I fold my arms and glare into the lens, my ribcage heaving. Right this second I want nothing more than to step into a chessboxing ring with that Day of the Dead pantomime ghoul and bash her like a piñata.

Kit waits a few more seconds, then cracks a smile. 'Nailed it,' he says. 'Absolutely nailed it.'

'Are you okay?' I pull him to his feet. 'I didn't plan to push you like that. It just happened.'

'I'm fine. It was a nice touch.'

'Should we do another take?'

'No. We've got what we need.' He flips his laptop open and hunts in his camera bag for a USB cable.

'Do you think it will get under her skin?'

'Nope.' Kit yanks a cable out of the bag. 'I think it'll shuck her skin clean off her body.'

VIRAL

The title of the video is short and simple: **Park Girl calls out Zelda Haas**. It's only three weeks since we put it up on YouTube but the view count has already exceeded the other Park Girl video.

Ahahaha, don't be too sore, Zelda. At least I've made you the center of attention. That's how you like it, right?

THE TAP ON THE SHOULDER

I'm down in Bert's Gym bashing a speeding leather bag when the tap on the shoulder comes.

'Leah Baxter, right?'

The voice is high and nasal like some dumbass cartoon character, but when I turn around the man before me is not at all what I expected. He looks about fifty years old with a square jaw, a tailored suit and a Breitling watch so glittery it hurts my eyes.

'Harold Spiegelman,' says the man. 'I'm what they call a matchmaker. I work for Jonny Diamond.'

'Never heard of him.'

'Then you've never been to Vegas, sweetie.'

'Oh, please.' I grab a towel. 'You sound like a bad parody of yourself.'

'Is that so?' The matchmaker chuckles and shakes his head. 'Well, you sound like you got enough attitude to sink a South Dakota dreadnought. Don't get me wrong, I like that. The fans will like it too. So here's the glad tidings, short and simple. Jonny H. Diamond is the biggest fight promoter in all of Vegas and he's had his eye on chessboxing ever since I showed him *Cold Equator* twelve years ago. The number one thinking sport combined with the number one fighting sport, what's not to like? Get the right fight card and the tickets will sell like hot gatsbies. But there's the rub, see? We never found two characters big enough for the Strip.'

'Pity.'

'Till now, that is.'

I look at him. 'You want to sign me for a fight?'

'No, Jonny wants to sign you for a fight. Leah "Park Girl" Baxter versus Zelda "The Reaper" Haas. Caesar's Palace, six months from now. Half a million dollars, winner takes all.'

'Has Haas agreed?'

Spiegelman laughs long and loud. 'Has Haas agreed? You're quite something, kid. Haas *suggested* it.'

'Half a million dollars?' Mom and Clint are staring at me like I've transformed into a squirrel right here at the kitchen table. 'Half a million *American* dollars?'

'No, Tuvaluan dollars.' Silence. 'Yes, of course, American dollars. Bert looked over the contract for me and it all checks out just fine.'

Clint puffs out his cheeks. 'Whatever I may have said about chessboxing,' he grins, 'I take it all back.'

Mom scowls at him, then turns imploringly to me. 'You don't have to do this, Leah. We're proud of everything you've achieved in this hobby of yours, but perhaps it's gone far enough.'

'It's not a hobby, Mom. It's a lifesaver.' I lift my hand to stroke Anatoly, who is draped around my neck. 'You remember how I was after Dad died, right? Riddled with insecurity. Mad at everybody. Sabotaging myself at every turn. But going to Bert's Gym and getting into chessboxing, it's been good for me. I mean deep down good for me. I'm more positive now. I'm confident. The sadness is still there but I'm learning to live with it and that's certainly not because of Daphne All is Well Piano, it's because of my chessboxing. Do you think I'd be tutoring Teddy and those others if it wasn't for chessboxing? Do you think we'd even be having this conversation? Listen, I know you both think chessboxing is a dumbass sport. You're right, it is. But this dumbass sport has saved my life and that's a fact. Come to Vegas with me, Mom. You too, Clint. I'll make you both proud, I promise.'

Mom stares at me with tears in her eyes and heaves a ragged sigh. 'What's she called, this woman you're supposed to be fighting?'

'Zelda Haas.'

'H. A. A. S?' Mom has her phone out already and is pecking at the keypad.

'That's right,' I say. 'But I warn you Mom, she looks a little—'

Mom screams.

'Scary,' I mutter, too late.

Mom angles the phone toward me. Her hand is shaking. 'What's wrong with this woman, Leah? What could possess anyone to do that to themselves?'

'It's just her shtick,' I say, reaching out to swipe through the pictures. 'In Germany they call her the "Sensenfrau", the Grim Reaper.'

'I don't want you fighting that woman,' says Mom. 'Not for half a million dollars, not for a million dollars, not for all the money in the world. If a woman does that to her own face, who knows what else she's capable of?'

Clint puts his hand on Mom's. Their fingers interlace.

'Leah,' he says gently, 'I probably have no right to say this, but don't fight this woman to make your mom proud. Your mom is already proud of you, aren't you, Joanne?'

Mom nods mutely. A tear rolls down her cheek.

'And don't do it for the money,' continues Clint. 'Money's never a good reason to put yourself in harm's way.'

'Exactly,' croaks Mom.

'But at the same time' – Clint pauses, fumbling for words like a newbie Scrabble player – 'we understand what you just said about the sport feeling like a lifesaver. Don't we, Joanne?'

Mom clenches her jaw, squeezes her eyes tight shut and gives the most minuscule nod I've ever seen.

'And maybe' – Clint looks as uncomfortable as a patzer in zugzwang – 'maybe this is a battle you've got to fight. Isn't that right, Joanne?'

Mom pushes her chair back from the table and brandishes a finger in Clint's face. 'Stop putting words in my mouth!' she yells. 'If you really want to make yourself useful, go google flights to Vegas!'

Whap-whap-whap-whap. I'm at Bert's Gym, hammering the speed bag with alternating fists, scowling in concentration. Travis stands at my shoulder, checking my stance and counting time.

'You know what?' says Travis, breaking off his count. 'I think you're too obsessed with chessboxing. If you were a little less driven you'd have time for other things. Other people.'

'Probably.' I keep bashing the bag. 'And if you were a little *more* driven you'd have beaten Kreshnik Paloka.' It's a low blow, but it's true.

Travis blinks. 'Screw you,' he says.

He grabs his gym bag and leaves without looking back.

LAS VEGAS

Jonny Diamond stages the Haas–Baxter press conference on the Omnia's *Midsummer Night's Dream* patio terrace overlooking the Strip. We sit at a long checkered trestle table draped with promotional logos. Diamond in the middle, then me, then two suits from the World Chessboxing Organization, then dear old Marcus Crockett on the end. Cameramen and sports reporters gossip and fidget as they wait for the questions to begin.

The chair to the right of Jonny Diamond is empty. *Don't worry, folks*, he chuckles. *Death will be with us before you know it.*

It is a beautiful, clear night. I keep craning my neck to look at all the famous hotels and casinos along the Strip: The Mirage, The Linq, the Flamingo, Margaritaville, and towering above it all that iconic Eiffel Tower replica in the middle of Paris Las Vegas. Flashing lights and razzle-dazzle as far as the eye can see. Incredible.

Squinting past the fluorescent camera lights, I notice a dark-robed figure appear behind the press pack. She carries a glinting scythe – nothing plastic about it – and her face is shrouded by a wide black hood. Reporters and cameramen scramble to attention, half rising from their chairs. *Zelda!* they cry. *Look this way, Zelda!*

The Sensenfrau stalks wordlessly toward her chair, lays the scythe on the table and lifts ghost-white arms to pull back her hood.

The reporters gasp. One screams. The Reaper's eye sockets are empty.

She turns slowly and looks at me. I pick up a bottle of *Tahoe Springs* mineral water from the table and take a long swig, forcing myself to meet Death's gaze. Cameras flash. Blood pumps in my ears. I have heard of people having the whites of their eyes tattooed but have never seen it for myself. She must have done it recently.

The reporters clamor for Haas's attention. The first few questions are all for her:

How does it feel to have black dye injected into your eyes?

The Sensenfrau does not feel pain.

Does it scare people on the bus?

The Sensenfrau does not use public transport.

Are you looking forward to tomorrow's fight?

The Sensenfrau's job is to collect souls. Tomorrow she will collect another one.

How long will the contest be?

Long enough to make her suffer.

Is Leah Baxter the most talented chess player you have ever faced?

The child is mortal. The Sensenfrau feels nothing but pity for mortals.

I roll my eyes at her answers but in truth the fear is scrabbling into me hard and I can't stop it. *She's a screw-up,* I keep telling myself. *A crackpot. A freak. Injecting black ink into her eyes doesn't improve her chess or her right hook one little bit.*

Does it?

'Dressing room number two,' says Donna, standing aside to let me go in. 'You've got it to yourself so make yourself at home. If you need anything, just shout. I'll be right outside the door.'

Donna is one of the hospitality stewards at the Omnia. I'm still not old enough to enter a club on my own, so Donna has been assigned to escort me before and after the fight.

'Thanks,' I mutter. 'It's nice in here.'

Nice is an understatement. Ornate mirrors, plush carpets, framed photographs of singers and dancers, it's the swankiest prep room I've ever had.

'Oh, and one other thing,' says Donna, backing out of the room. 'After the contest, do try to bleed in the sink and not on the carpet. It's wool, you see.'

On my own at last, I unzip my sports bag and lay out my kit. Blue socks. Blue shorts. Hand wraps. Phone. Blue shirts. Blue gloves. High tops. Knife. Tape. Mouthpiece. Jump rope. Spare mouthpiece. Electric-blue silk robe with lightning bolts down the sides. Water bottles. Small glass bottle of Clubman aftershave.

Tahoe Springs says the label on the water bottles. Same brand they had on the table at the press conference last night. I open a bottle and take a sip. I can't help replaying the nightmare in my mind. *The Sensenfrau's job is to collect souls. Tomorrow she collects another one . . .*

I blink twice and glance up at a clock on the wall. *Stop thinking about last night*, I tell myself. *Remember Samuel Reshevsky. Fear no one.* I grab my penknife off the dressing room table and stab it into a bottle of *Tahoe Springs*, puncturing the cap. Then a second, then a third. Makes them easier to squirt.

We used to do the same at home when I was little. On hot summer days we'd collect up all our plastic bottles and Dad would use a hammer and nail to squirtify them. Sometimes he would shove a bike pump needle in the other end and make a proper water gun for me to run around with.

It is easy to underestimate how far a bike pump water gun can shoot, especially when you're seven years old. One time, a slug of water sailed through a half-open window and splashed on Dad's computer. He rushed out the house and started yelling. I remember it clearly because I heard him say two words I'd never heard before, one of which was *motherboard*.

I remember it for another reason too. When Dad came out, his eyes looked strange. He wrenched the plastic water bottle out my hands and hit me with it hard. Twice on my head, then once on my back as I tried to run away.

At bedtime he kept saying *I'm sorry, Leah* and *Forgive me, Leah*, and I remained stubbornly silent because I preferred to hear him plead. At the time it felt like power of a sort.

I finish squirtifying my water bottles, then sit back in my chair and look at the clock. 'I forgive you, Dad,' I murmur.

A sudden ping from my phone makes me jump.

Hey, champ. I'd try the Kasparov Gambit tonight if I were you x

My fingers skitter over the keypad. **Mom, there's no such thing**.

Ping. **So much the better. You'll have surprise on your side x**

WELCOME TO THE OMNIA

I stand behind a velvet curtain in the wings of the Omnia Club. My hands are wrapped. My muscles are warm. I'm as ready as I will ever be.

The Omnia is a cavernous vaulted hall at least five times bigger than the Elephant Club, boasting tier upon tier of gold and purple viewing platforms that seem to float in mid-air. Reminds me of the Galactic Senate in *Star Wars*, except with softer furnishings and harder funk.

The viewing platforms overlook the floodlit boxing ring in the middle of the dance floor. Inside the ring, microphone raised to his lips, is Marcus Crockett, surrounded on all sides by rapt spectators. He looks tiny but the multi-million-dollar sound system makes him boom like Thor.

'Welcome to the Omnia, ladies and gentlemen, and welcome to the most Vegas spectacle ever invented, a rootin' tootin' Vladimir Putin of a sport, a mesmerizing mashup of mankind's most ancient sporting obsessions, chess and boxing. What you are about to see is the most hubristic battle ever waged on a stage: an audacious young hero from the Center of the Universe pitting her mind and body against the ultimate enemy, the Grim Reaper herself!'

Wave after wave of cheers and boos cascade down from the viewing platforms. I have no idea which platform Mom and Clint are on but wherever they are I'm pretty sure Mom has her fingers in her ears. *Why must the music be so loud, Clint?*

'Over the chessboard and in the ring the two contestants will pit their wits against each other until there is a winner by checkmate or knockout. Take your seats, ladies and gentlemen, for the craziest show in town. It's omnibulous. It's omnificent. It's Chessboxing at the Omnia!'

The music pulses to a crescendo and the entire ceiling lights up like a colossal chandelier, concentric oval rings that swirl in orange and blood red. I smooth the wrappings on my hands and bounce on the balls of my feet.

Dad, I mouth. *Help me.*

'Fighting out of the blue corner, official weight 129 pounds, a girl with a million hits and a billion burns, please welcome the Whirlwind of Washington Square, the Hellcat of Hell's

Kitchen, Supreme Ruler of the Fiefdom of Feist, our very own haymaking, checkmating, face-breaking, fate-baiting trailblazer Leah "Park Girl" Baxter!'

I step out onto the catwalk and stride toward the boxing ring with my fists in the air and my electric-blue silk robe swishing around my body.

Floodlights bright enough to blow your vision out. Favela funk fit to make Satan cry. The crowd so close and loud it feels like they're inside me. Shouts of 'Park Girl' and 'Leah!' and one dumb squawk that sounds like 'Marry me!'

'Ladies and gentlemen, fighting out of the red corner, all the way from Berlin, Germany, official weight 130 pounds, put your affairs in order and hang onto your souls because here comes the heat-seeking, havoc-wreaking, unspeaking, unyielding, scythe-wielding Women's Chessboxing Champion of the World, Zelda "the Reaper" Haaaaaas!'

A fog cannon blasts and all the lights go out, except for the flashing lights in the chandelier above our heads. The crowd screams and whoops as the chandelier spins and comes apart, unfurling eight concentric rings of hi-tech awesomeness. Each segment moves independently of the next, spinning and tilting and descending toward us like a spaceship about to land.

I am Death, booms a voiceover. *I have walked by your side for quite some time and now at last we shall meet face to face. Are you ready, mortal?*

The lights flood back on, and there in the middle of the ring not fifteen feet away from me is the Grim Reaper herself. Screams of horror fill the air as the Sensenfrau raises her scythe and pulls back her dark hood. Her skin is white as leprosy, her eye sockets as black as night.

How did she get there? Syd and I kept saying that to each other last fall as we watched her footwork on YouTube. *How did she get there? How did she move so fast? It's like she can teleport from place to place. Maybe she really is the Grim Reaper.*

It's just her shtick, I tell myself, but my blood is thick and cold and the fear is scratching deep into my soul.

ROUND 1

I take my seat across the board from Death. Everything around me is ultra HD. I see the contours of each knight and bishop in astounding detail, the crease of the referee's Oxford collar, the sheen of the chess clock, the fine weave of my hand wraps, the glint of a dime as it spins in the air.

Remember Reshevsky.

Fear no one.

Haas wins the toss and chooses White. The instant her clock begins to tick, the vastness of the Omnia contracts to a span of sixty-four black and white squares.

Pawn c4.
Knight f6.
Knight f3.

Czechoslovakian grandmaster Richard Reti was the first person to beat Capa after Capa became world champion. Back in the day, Reti's opening strategy for White was groundbreaking. Allow Black to occupy the center of the board and then attack like crazy on both flanks. Not so groundbreaking these days, of course. If the Reaper won't occupy the center, I'll happily take it for myself.

I push my d pawn two squares forward. Death stares at the move with empty eyes. She would have expected the more common moves e6 or g6. Probably had a ton of opening theory memorized. *Take that, Skullface. Two moves in, you're already in the woods.*

Pawn g3. Bishop f5.

Pawn takes pawn. Knight takes pawn.

That's good. The central tension is broken and we're in for a nice open position with plenty of tactical—

What have I done? What have I done? I've left myself open to pawn e4, forking my knight and my bishop. I looked at e4 earlier and of course I discounted it because the bishop simply takes, but here's the thing — if my bishop does take, there's a brutal follow-up fork, queen a4, checking my king and winning a bishop. It's more than a neat combo, it's a killer blow, *on the fifth freaking move of the game.*

Calm down, I tell myself. *Don't show her you're rattled. She hasn't played e4 yet. Perhaps she hasn't spotted it.* But one glance at Haas tells me she has. She's sitting back in her chair, not looking at the board at all, just gazing at me with that horrible death's head grin of hers. She knows this line inside out. If she hasn't yet played e4 it's because she wants to enjoy the moment. She wants to sit and grin a little longer. She wants to watch me suffer.

Marcus Crockett looks like he's talking fast into his mic, obviously trying to explain this car crash of an opening to a disbelieving crowd. An early defeat is bad not just for me but also for the sport. People have paid good money to watch a spectacle worthy of Las Vegas and already the match is as good as over.

Death reaches out and nudges her king's pawn to e4, exactly the move I dreaded. I take it with my bishop – I have no choice – and quick as a flash she plays the follow-up fork, queen to a4.

Chessmen swirl before my eyes. I feel sick. All of that training and preparation, only to fall prey to an opening trap straight out of some dumbass *Win With the Reti* book.

I block the check with my queenside knight and then in deliberate slow-motion Haas slides her queen along the fourth rank to capture my bishop. She leers at the crowd and lifts the stricken bishop high above her head like some evil priestess presenting a still-beating human heart to a throng of ghouls. My headphones muffle the resulting cheer but I can see the excitement in the crowd. Jaws drop, drinks spill, fists punch the air. First blood to the Sensenfrau.

My head is in my hands. I'm staring at the board, willing it to reveal a shred of positional compensation for my loss, but there is none. Just the gaping emptiness of that c8-h3 diagonal where my light-squared bishop once held sway. The captured bishop is right there by my opponent's elbow and the gash in his mitre looks for all the world like a groaning mouth. *I'm dead*, wails the mouth. *I'm never coming back*. The feeling of shock and disbelief at losing a piece so prematurely, it's like a sort of grief.

A sudden commotion pierces my despair. The chessboard is gone from in front of me, and the table too. I take off my headphones. Favela funk and catcalls assault my ears.

'. . . facing a real uphill battle on the chessboard,' Crockett is saying, 'but let's see what she can do in the ring.'

ROUND 2

I lurch to my feet and pull my gloves over my bandaged hands. A card girl prances around the ring in high heels. The referee motions for us to come together. The bell rings, the crowd roars and a red glove punches me in the face.

I'm stunned, not by the punch but by what just happened on the board. *Bishop f5, that was the blunder. It seemed like an obvious developing move, the sort of move you don't think twice about—*

Oof! Another jab to the face. I reel away and raise my guard, but Death is coming after me and she's backing me up fast and hard and if I don't start concentrating right this second I'm going to get steamrollered.

We clinch. I breathe. Death leans in close and whispers in my ear, 'What a pity about your bishop. No Boden's mate tonight, or?'

I attempt an uppercut to her liver, but my arm is half-pinned and the blow has no force. We spin apart and circle each other at range. Death gazes on me with empty eyes.

Remember the plan, I tell myself. *Work the body shots. Do the kind of damage that will cost her in the later rounds.* I step forward and throw a straight right to her body, but her body is no longer in front of me, it's beside me, and it's me who's stumbling sideways to escape from a barrage of punches. *It's like she can teleport from place to place.*

Nothing sinister, I tell myself. *Just good technique. Whatever you do, don't turtle up.* But it's too late, because Death is backing me up again with a five, six, seven-punch combo, and I'm slumping on the ropes with nothing in my field of vision but the pure mad menace of her eyes.

ROUND 3

The table, chairs and chessboard reappear and the nightmare of my position confronts me anew. A bishop down with no positional advantage. I should resign right now and save myself a slow humiliating death.

I reach out to topple my king but my hand freezes in mid-air and in my mind I'm at Number 23 West 10th Street, sitting on the wall with a nine-year-old boy.

Resigning is for wimps, Teddy. Take a leaf from Frank Marshall's book. Dig deep. Find a way back.

Dig deep. It sounds so easy. Wasn't so easy for Teddy Croft when he went to Richmond five months ago and competed in the Under-ten Nationals. Wasn't so easy for Teddy Croft when he lost six games out of six, poor kid, and had to play each one through to its agonizing finish just cos some girl once sat him on a wall and spewed Frank Marshall psychobabble all over him.

I grab a knight and move it to f6. The only reason I'm not resigning is because of Teddy. I streamed the Richmond games on my phone and watched him get gutted six times in succession. If I get gutted once, so be it. It's what I deserve.

Death glides her queen back to a4. I move a pawn to block the check.

d pawn forward. e pawn forward.

Queenside knight. Kingside bishop.

I'm going to lose this game sooner or later but at least I can make Death work for her victory. I'll be the terrier that won't let go, the fly that refuses to be swatted. What was it Kasparov used to say? *It is when working under limitations that the master reveals himself.*

Haas strokes the hinge of her tattooed jaw and lashes out with pawn h4. I haven't even castled yet and already she's coming for my king. It's a kickass move, just the sort of thing I would have played myself in her position. But like all kingside pawn moves, it has also created a tiny weakness, something for me to aim at.

Queen c7. Knight takes knight.

Pawn takes knight. Bishop g2.

I lick my dry, cracked lips. If I were playing a patzer in the park I know exactly what I would do right now. I would sac my dark-squared bishop like a shot and send my queen marauding. But Haas is no patzer and I can't see my way to a sure-fire mating net. I'd be two bishops down with nothing to show for it.

What the heck, I'll do it anyways. Give the crowd a thrill and go down fighting.

I reach out my right hand and instantly my head fills up with noise and crunching gears.

Cry me a river in Memphis Mall
Molotov Me will sabotage it all!

I draw back my hand and lift my face to the angry chandelier and out of my abdomen and up through my throat and out of my mouth comes a scream of grief and rage so powerful that even the immense Omnia cannot contain it, nor Caesar's Palace, nor Las Vegas, nor the Grand Canyon, nor the lone and level sands of the Nevada Desert.

Do you hear that, Death? I refuse. I will not sabotage myself. That bishop stays where it is. I will sit on my hands to stop myself touching it and I will dig deep and I will find a way back. You watch.

ROUND 4

Death dances toward me with red boxing gloves and we exchange a flurry of jabs and crosses. *Stop looking at the punches,* I remind myself. *Look past the punches. Keep your eyes on her upper chest. Make sure you always know where she is.*

We clinch. I try to breathe, but Death's free right hand is pecking at my liver. *Peck. Peck. Peck.*

'That was quite a scream,' she whispers.

I twist out of the clinch and back away.

Stick with the game plan. Footwork and body shots. Tire her out. Mess with her mind. Wait till the eighth round when her limbs are slow and heavy and she can't teleport no more. Then and only then I'll move inside and pound her like a nail.

ROUND 5

I bite down hard on my lower lip and stare at the chessboard, gazing deep into my hopeless position. The bishop sac still looks tempting, and still I refuse it. Even Mikhail Tal would not go two bishops down without a sure-fire advantage to be gained.

I reach out, castle on the kingside and tap the clock.

Death smiles. Her flank pawn marches on, puncturing my kingside defenses. The breach is bad but not fatal. My king still has protectors.

On move nineteen Death lapses into thought for what seems like an eternity. Second by second her clock ticks down and still she does nothing. What is she thinking about? Has her attack run out of steam or is she messing with my head? Perhaps she has died and rigor mortis is setting in.

No such luck. Death is alive. She's moving a knight. To e5, *where I can take it with a pawn.*

I stare down at the knight, then up at the Reaper. Even at master level idiotic blunders do happen occasionally. You think for so long that you psych yourself out and you end up making a move of patzeresque stupidity. *But wait, is this a blunder or a Trojan horse? Beware of Death, even bearing gifts.*

My delight turns gradually to dread. The knight advance is not a gift, not by any stretch.

If I ignore the knight, she exchanges on e4 and her queen goes to b3, re-entering the fray with devastating effect. If I take it with my bishop, she liquidates quickly to a won endgame. If I play the obvious move and take the knight with my pawn? Sure, I win back the material I blundered at the beginning of the game, but at what cost? Bishop to f6, that's what, and then rook h7 check, a textbook skewer. The rook forces my king to move aside, then captures the queen beyond.

Death stares at me with a scornful half-smile. Our eyes meet and she nods almost imperceptibly. It's like she can see right into my mind. She can see that I've spotted the skewer and she can see how much it scares me.

ROUND 6

Black-eyed and red-gloved, Death comes for me again. I tuck in my elbows and concentrate on my footwork, surfing back and forth like a clam in a current. My guard is up but she's jabbing hard and fast, pushing my own gloves right into my face.

I skip back out of range. *Footwork and body shots*, I remind myself. *Mess with her mind. Tire her out.*

Yet again she sails toward me. I bob. I weave. A straight right flies over my shoulder. I counter low down, *crack*, and hear the gasp.

She felt that.

I spin off to my left, bouncing on quick feet, probing the space between us with my jab.

Same again, I tell myself. *Footwork and body shots. Do the kind of damage that will cost her in the later rounds.*

Already Haas is moving more slowly and breathing heavily. Her left hand is high but the right is down by her side, cradling her liver. I hurt her.

I bounce forward, bobbing and weaving. Death cowers and backs off, shrinking into herself, as black-eyed and tightly coiled as a royal python. The corner of her mouth twitches.

What's that? A smile?

It's too late to pull the punch. My right cross whistles over Death's head, leaving my upper ribcage and armpit horribly exposed. I'm pitching forward and she is rising to meet me. *Shoop!* she delivers a cruel uppercut straight into my armpit.

A flash of hard white pain radiates through my chest cavity. My head hits the canvas. The chandelier wheels and tilts above me, red and orange like blood and tongues of fire.

Cheers and groans ring in my ears. The ref is already halfway through his count. *Four. Five. Six.*

'Come on, champ!'

That wild shriek was not the referee. I twist my neck. Far up and to my right I see a spot of emerald velour and peroxide hair.

Mom!

I roll onto my front, grab the ropes and heave with all my broken might.

I stand at the chessboard crying. It hurts too much to sit. The pain across my ribcage is unbearable.

The spectators have gone very still. What's wrong with them? Isn't this what they paid to watch? Blood and tears dripping on a chessboard?

The ringside doctor is leaning over the ropes, trying to attract the attention of the match referee.

Racked with pain I lift my thumb. *I'm good.*

I bite down hard on my mouth guard and force myself to focus past the pain and concentrate on this white knight that has ridden so heroically and absurdly into the heart of my defenses. What is to be done about it?

I close my eyes, visualize the position after bishop f6 and start to map the garden. First off, I could avoid the wicked skewer by playing queen c8. *Does it work? Does it work? Does it work? Does it work?* No. Five moves down the line Haas wins a rook for a bishop and emerges into a won endgame.

Find something else. Find something better.

Minutes tick by. Deeper and deeper I map the forking paths five moves, ten moves, twenty moves deep. I'm taking tiny shallow breaths because I still can't manage a full one. *Are my ribs broken*, I wonder, *or just badly bruised?*

How about this? Allow the skewer. Let her win my queen. An uncomfortable line to consider, but the more I look at it, the more playable it looks. I get a bishop and a rook in exchange for the queen and eventually I can secure good outposts for my remaining pieces. Squirrel the king away on g7, bishop on b6, double up my rooks behind the e pawn. I'll still be losing, but for the first time in the game I'll have decent prospects of a counterattack. And the further up the board I advance that e pawn, the more powerful it becomes.

I open my eyes. I have spent the entire chess round thinking about a single move, and the line I've chosen is the very one Haas thought I would avoid at all costs. I grab my f pawn and capture that benighted knight so hard it flies right off the table.

Haas shakes her head and hunches forward over the board, but before she can start thinking, a stagehand stops the clocks and whisks the chessboard away.

Death slaps the table in frustration. There's nothing so hard to win as a won game.

ROUND 8

The lights on the spaceship pulse and flash. A card girl sashays around the ring. Round 8.

I'll wait till the eighth round when her limbs are slow and heavy and she can't teleport no more. Then and only then I'll move inside and pound her like a nail.

The crucial round has arrived. My weary eyes scan the viewing platforms, searching for a patch of emerald velour, to no avail. The bruise under my right arm is turning purple and I'm struggling to get my right glove on.

The bell rings.

I fasten the velcro around my wrist. Death skips toward me and this time I don't step back.

I step forward.

I throw a jab. Death counters. I counter the counter. She counters that.

Mom's voice rends the air, loud and anguished. 'I love you, Leah!'

Counter counter counter counter counter counter counter counter counter counter

I love you, Leah.

Counter counter

I love you, Leah.

Counter! Counter! The simultaneous double punch rips a hole in the fight and we both fall backward onto the canvas, like Accident Amy running into a mirror.

Dad loved Accident Amy running into that mirror. He laughed so hard he snorted root beer out his nose.

We sit up. Death looks at me and spits a tooth. Her eyes are expressionless but her tattooed lips are a window on her soul.

She's furious.

ROUND 9

Death exchanges on e4 as I knew she would, then slides her bishop to f6. As I knew she would.

I bash out king f7 lightning fast. When you play instant moves in a complex situation, it saps your opponent's confidence. It forces them to go back and reanalyze everything they thought they knew.

Death thinks for a long time, then goes ahead and plays the skewer on h7, but she does it hesitantly, almost reluctantly. She has now realized, her skewer is not the game winner she thought it was.

A flurry of exchanges, a few cunning checks from my opponent's queen and then the dust settles. My king is safe for now on g7, my bishop is on b6, my rooks are on e6 and e8. The Reaper has her nose in front, but she's going to need some sharp positional play to keep it there, and the correct moves in this position are far from obvious.

Her shoulders have slumped. Her expression is sullen. She glances irritably at the clock and probes the position for a way to convert her advantage into a win. At long last she reaches out and pushes her Gambler to a3.

Suboptimal, surely. The pawn push on the flank is a waiting move, a nothing, a passing of the buck. In a position like this, initiative is everything. You can't afford to be passive.

That one moment of hesitation has shifted the balance of play in my favor.

I lean forward hungrily and advance my e pawn. Death plays rook d7 to force a rook exchange, then queen b4 to threaten my remaining rook. If I scurry to defend, I lose the initiative. There must be something better . . .

And there is. I push my e pawn once again. Check.

Death plays king e1, blocking the march of my pawn. She thinks she has thwarted my attack, but she's wrong. I'm not done yet. At last it's time to sac that bishop.

The Reaper watches helplessly as the kamikaze cleric glides down its diagonal and captures the footsoldier on f2. Check. There it is again, the lip curl of frustration. She has no choice but to accept the sacrifice although she knows full well what happens when she does.

The humble pawn becomes a queen.

ROUND 10

Death charges toward me with a left-lead haymaker. I slip underneath it, step to the left and tag her *Yop!* on her jagged nose tattoo. She goes down clutching her face. The crowd whoop and holler. Even the bottle service customers are on their feet.

She gets up, snorts and comes at me again. This is the last of the maximum five boxing rounds so she needs a knockout fast. She's bobbing and weaving, searching for one big hook that will spin my brain inside my head and put my ass to sleep.

Me, I just keep going as best I can. Keep my hands up. Keep slipping and rolling. Keep drilling her with short hard jabs and uppercuts. Keep her on her heels.

We clinch. Death feels cool and slick with sweat. She reaches gently around toward my back and side and *Crack!* I'm down on one knee.

The ref bounds in. Kidney punches are illegal. Death is on an official warning.

Like Death cares.

Again she comes for me. Again I jab. She counters with a wild right hand, her head goes back and *Glop!* I hit her in the throat. Death's mouthpiece shoots out of her mouth and bounces on the canvas. She doubles over, gasping for air.

And I'm gasping too, because I just realized something.

I'm going to win.

ROUND 11

The chessboard reappears. There is a deep cut on my forehead. Warm blood is trickling down into my left eye.

Someone hands me a gauze pad. The referee starts the clocks.

I press the pad to my head with my left hand and move the pieces with my right, smashing out the exchanges hard and fast. King takes bishop. Pawn promotes. Queen takes queen. Rook takes queen. King takes rook.

We've reached the endgame and I am totally winning. To the patzers in the crowd my advantage might not look significant. One extra pawn on the queenside and a marginally more active king. But as Marcus Crockett must be explaining to them, the extra pawn and the one square head start for my king will soon make all the difference in this game.

I know it. Marcus Crockett knows it. Most importantly, Death knows it. She pulls her lip distractedly and glances in desperation at the clocks. She has two minutes left for all of her moves, and I have forty-two seconds. She pushes a pawn to b4 and slaps her timer.

Click-clack, click-clack, the moves flow fast and furious like a Saturday afternoon in the park. I bring my king to the center, advance my g pawn, lure the white king toward the kingside, then change direction and head for the queenside pawns. *Click-clack*, gobble-gobble, thank you very much. I now have three passed pawns, an unstoppable platoon.

The white king scurries for the corner, hoping I will blunder into a stalemate. Desperate stuff from Death.

Clickety-clack, clickety-clack, I flush the king from its hiding place and start promoting pawns. If this were a tournament game I would use two queens to finish her swiftly. But this is Vegas and this is Death and I have a sweeter end in mind. I'm going to use three bishops to deliver the most humiliating checkmate in chess history.

My Innkeeper pawn is home. I grab one of my dead bishops and slam it down on the promotion square. *Resurrection!*

The Gambler is next – another bishop. Crockett is laughing into his mic as he conveys this madness to the crowd. You hardly ever see bishop promotions in tournament chess. Certainly not in high stakes blitz with twenty-five seconds left on the clock.

There are only two black bishops in a normal chess set so promoting my Guard is tricky. The ref has to stop the clocks while a stagehand rushes off to find an extra bishop backstage. By now Marcus Crockett is laughing too hard to commentate and Zelda Haas is on her feet yelling like a banshee. The ref waves away her protests. Everything I am doing is legal.

The extra bishop arrives and the ref restarts the clocks. Three cheeky clergymen strobe the board in fabulous formations. Haas heads for the corner, still hoping for a chance stalemate, but that corner is exactly where I want her. I put two dark-squared bishops as baulkheads on e3 and e5 and then, with seven seconds left on my clock, I slam the light-squared bishop onto e4, impaling the white king right through the middle of its crown.

Checkmate.

I remove my headphones and offer to shake but Haas ignores my hand. I turn my back on her, run to the corner of the ring and leap up onto the ropes, throwing my arms wide. Pyrotechnics explode around the ring. The crowd roars its delight.

Chessboxing Champion of the World. The pain is gone, all gone, and I feel so happy I could die.

I imagine that Dad is way up high in one of the bottle service pods. I visualize him climbing over the parapet and shinning down the lighting rig toward me. I imagine throwing myself off the apron of the boxing ring and crowd-surfing toward him. Gliding into his outstretched arms. Clinging to him. I feel the scratchiness of his brown woolen jacket and smell once more the musky, citric scent of Clubman aftershave.

'Well done, champ!' he screams in my ear. 'I knew you could do it! Every time you went down, I knew you'd get up. Every time Death hit you, I knew you'd bounce back. Even when you doubted yourself, I never did. Not for one moment.'

END

There's not much more to say about that night. Fact is, my celebrations were cut short by the wound above my eye suddenly gaping open again. One moment I'm standing on the ropes with my arms in the air feeling like half a million dollars and the next moment there's horror on the faces of the ringside fans and warm blood flowing into my left eye like the freakin' Mississippi. The ringside doctor made me sit down at the chessboard while she tried to close the cut with butterfly strips.

After that it's all kind of hazy.

I remember the roar of the crowd as Marcus Crockett thrust my fist into the air.

I remember a brief glimpse of emerald velour.

And I remember that crazy chandelier wheeling up, up and away into space.

TWENTY-FOUR HOURS

'Hello, champ!' calls a familiar voice.

I open my eyes, blinking and scowling in the bright light. Mom sashays toward my bed in a cream trouser suit, a Sahel bag over her arm.

'Where am I?' I groan.

'B ward, Sunrise Hospital, downtown Vegas.' Mom passes me a glass of water. 'The doctors patched you up a treat last night, Leah. Twelve stitches above your eye and cold compresses everywhere else. They want to keep you in for another twenty-four hours, though. They're worried about concussion.'

'Twenty-four hours!' I groan. 'What am I supposed to do for twenty-four hours?'

'I don't know.' Mom swipes a track on my cell and hands me my earbuds. 'Just lie back, I guess, and listen to Mahler.'

Okay, dear readers, I get it. You wanted the Sensenfrau to knock me senseless. You wanted to see my prodigious brain spattered all over the Omnia.

Well, too bad. I'm alive-alive-o, and I'm celebrating being alive by putting this whole dumbass journal online. I know, I know, humungous overshare, but I've decided everything in life is better with a bit of kibitzing. Besides, it may help you to know that there's someone out there even more screwed up than you are.

COMMENTS 💬

Juna: Congratulations! Women's Chessboxing Champion of the World. Go you!

Gorgon: Just watched the bout on YouTube. Epic isn't the word. Congratulations!

Chessgirl: Thank you!

SirLancelot: Congrats! Btw, you never got back to me about those chess books. Do you still need them?

Chessgirl: Yes, I do. Sorry.

Guppy: Congratulations and all that. I've been looking at your game and I think you'll find that instead of playing d5 on move 2, you should have played g6, preparing to fianchetto your king's bishop. That's the most common Anglo-Indian setup.

Sigurd: She didn't want the most common setup, dumbass. She played d5 to get away from the book lines.

Guppy: d5 is already a book line. It's just not a very good one, as evidenced by her going a bishop down after four moves. So mind who you're calling dumbass, dumbass.

Sigurd: d5 was fine. Her only mistake was playing bishop f5 when she should have exchanged on c4. You clearly have the IQ of lint, so please don't comment further.

Guppy: Let's play horse. I'll be the front end and you be yourself.

Sigurd: *This comment has been removed by the moderator.*

Guppy: *This comment has been removed by the moderator.*

Comments on this post are now closed.

STITCHES

On my second morning in hospital, Clint shows up. He tells me and Mom that there are lots of people at the front desk, all clamoring for a piece of me.

'Who are they?' I ask.

Clint thumbs through a small pile of business cards. 'Jonny Diamond. Harold Spiegelman. A bunch of reporters and photographers. Bloggers. Good-looking boy called Seb with a camera strapped to his head. Oh, and a rather odd character called Kim or Kip or something. He didn't have a card.'

'Kit!' I turn to Mom. 'He's a friend of mine. Can I see him?'

'All right.' Mom sighs. 'But just a short visit, Leah. You need to conserve your strength.'

Clint goes out to fetch Kit, and I sit up in bed, wincing at the pain across my ribcage.

'I love the moment when I crush a man's ego!' Bobby pipes up suddenly.

I grab my cell off the nightstand. It's Travis, calling to congratulate me on the win. He tells me that Bert set up a projector in the gym and they streamed the whole thing on pay-per-view.

'You're kidding,' I reply. 'The bout didn't even start till midnight Eastern Time.'

'I know, right?' Travis laughs. 'Some of the folks in the second-floor apartments came down to complain about the noise and they ended up staying to watch. There must have been about twenty-five of us leaping around in front of that screen. I told them it was me who got you into chessboxing in the first place.'

'Well, I'm glad they got that straight.' I can hear footsteps in the corridor outside. 'Listen, Travis, I've got to go. Goodbye.'

The door opens and a pair of twinkling blue eyes appear.

'Kit!' Joy rises in my aching chest.

'How now!' he yells, skipping over to Mom and bowing low. 'Thou art thy daughter's glass,' he purrs, 'and she in thee calls back the lovely April of your prime.'

Mom smiles uncertainly and looks at me for help.

'Mom, this is Kit McTarnsay,' I say. 'Don't worry, he's always like this. His grandfather was a famous Irish poet, or so he claims.' Kit bounds to my bedside and I lean forward to hug him tight. 'What are you doing here?' I ask. 'I thought you hated chessboxing.'

'I do.'

'So why did you watch it?'

'I didn't. I had my hands over my eyes most of the time. But I was in the venue and that's what counts, right?'

'Sure, I'm really touched. How could you afford—'

'I had a few ducats left over from my Poisoned Pawn days. Can we not talk about money, though? It's unseemly.'

'Okay. What should we talk about?'

Kit brushes his hair behind his ears and looks at me tenderly. 'I don't know. Chess?'

COMMENTS

Gorgon: Do you still want to get that tattoo?

Chessgirl: Not just yet. I'm sure you understand.

Hamsterlover: How's Teddy doing?

Chessgirl: I don't know. After what happened at the Nationals, he told his parents he prefers Hungry Hippos to chess. I don't blame him. I kind of wish I'd played more Hungry Hippos when I was nine.

Lisa: Are you going to keep seeing Daphne Piano?

Chessgirl: Sure, why not? She loves our little chats.

Skipperbekker: When do you think you'll get over your dad's death?

Chessgirl: Honestly? Never. It's a half-stitched scar and always will be. Learning to encompass the grief, though, that'd be something. I've definitely made a start.

Roy: So, what's next for Leah 'Park Girl' Baxter?

Chessgirl: I'm not sure. I know it sounds crazy but I've got this itch to return to tournament chess. Nineteen's not ancient, right?

QWERTY1: This is the last year you'll be eligible for the World Junior Chess Tournament. The winner gets a GM title automatically. Why not go for that?

Chessgirl: Wait a second. Is that you, Mom?

QWERTY1: Haha, no.

Anonymous: Do your sneezes still sound like coughs?

Chessgirl: Yes. But you know what? There are weirdos out there who will bless you even for coughing.

ACKNOWLEDGEMENTS

I wrote most of this book in Battersea Reference Library in London. The room has oak paneling around the walls and a glazed vault supported by cast-iron columns. Carved above the entrance is Battersea's motto: NON MIHI, NON TIBI, SED NOBIS.

Not me, not you, but us. It's an apt motto, not just for Battersea but also for this book. I am indebted to my agent, Julia Churchill, whose enthusiasm for the characters sustained me through several rewrites, and to my editor Chloe Sackur, whose wise advice resulted in a far better story than I could ever have written alone.

AFTERWORD

Each square on a chessboard is identified by a letter and a number, for example e2 or g5.

The vertical columns of squares (called files) are labelled a to h.

The horizontal rows of squares (called ranks) are numbered 1 to 8.

N	knight
B	bishop
R	rook
Q	queen
K	king
e4	pawn moves to e4
exd5	e pawn captures on d5
Qxd5	queen captures on d5
Nc3	knight to c3
N7f6	knight on seventh rank moves to f6
Rfe8	rook on f file moves to e8
e1=Q	e pawn promotes to queen

+	check	
#	checkmate	
1-0	White wins	
0-1	Black wins	
?	mistake	
??	blunder	
!	very good move	
!!	brilliant move	

GAME 1

Leah's game against Odette Segal followed the same moves as a spectacular 1934 game played by Peruvian master Esteban Canal. White sacrifices two rooks and a queen in order to force Boden's mate on the fourteenth move.

Baxter-Segal, New York, Scandinavian Opening

1. e4 d5	6. Bf4 e6	11. axb4!! Qxa1+
2. exd5 Qxd5	7. h3 Bxf3	12. Kd2! Qxh1
3. Nc3 Qa5	8. Qxf3 Bb4	13. Qxc6+! bxc6
4. d4 c6	9. Be2 Nd7	14. Ba6# 1–0
5. Nf3 Bg4	10. a3 0-0-0	

GAME 2

The opening trap from Leah's game against Zelda Haas was played by Zaitsik in a 1976 game against Zichulidze. In that game Black resigned on move 5. I used a chess engine

called Stockfish to imagine how Black might have dug deep
and found a way back.

Haas-Baxter, Las Vegas, Reti Opening

1. c4 Nf6
2. Nf3 d5
3. g3 Bf5??
4. cxd5 Nxd5
5. e4! Bxe4
6. Qa4+ Nd7
7. Qxe4 N7f6
8. Qa4+ c6
9. d4 e6
10. Nc3 Bd6
11. h4 Qc7
12. Nxd5 exd5
13. Bg2 O-O
14. Bg5 Rfe8+
15. Kf1 Ne4
16. h5 f6
17. Bh4 g5
18. hxg6 hxg6
19. Ne5 fxe5
20. Bxe4 dxe4
21. Bf6 Kf7
22. Rh7+ Kxf6
23. Rxc7 Bxc7

24. dxe5+ Rxe5
25. Qb4 Bb6
26. Qd6+ Re6
27. Qf4+ Kg7
28. Rd1 Rae8
29. a3? e3
30. Rd7+ R6e7
31. Rxe7+ Rxe7
32. Qb4 e2+
33. Ke1 Bxf2+
34. Kxf2 e1=Q+
35. Qxe1 Rxe1
36. Kxe1 Kf6
37. b4 Ke5
38. Ke2 Ke4
39. a4 g5
40. Kf2 g4
41. Ke2 a6
42. Kf2 Kd3
43. a5 Kc4
44. Ke3 Kxb4
45. Kd3 c5
46. Kc2 c4

47. Kd2 Kxa5
48. Kc3 b5
49. Kb2 Kb4
50. Kc1 Kb3
51. Kb1 c3
52. Kc1 a5
53. Kb1 a4
54. Kc1 a3
55. Kd1 c2+
56. Kd2 a2
57. Ke3 a1=B
58. Kf4 c1=B+
59. Kxg4 b4
60. Kh5 Kc4
61. g4 b3
62. g5 b2
63. g6 b1=B
64. g7 Bxg7
65. Kg4 Bh7
66. Kg3 B1h6
67. Kg2 Be3
68. Kh2 Be5+
69. Kh1 Be4#

BLOOD & INK

STEPHEN DAVIES

Kadija is the music-loving daughter of a guardian of the
sacred manuscripts of the ancient city of Timbuktu, Mali.
Ali is a former shepherd boy, trained as a warrior for Allah.
Tonight, the Islamist rebels are coming for Timbuktu. They
will install a harsh regime of law and tear apart the peaceful
world within the mud walls of the city. Television, football,
radios, even music, will be banned.

Kadija refuses to let go of her
former life. And something in
her defiance draws Ali to her.
Which path will he choose?

'An exciting combination of
sweeping romance, adventure,
danger and history'
INIS

9781783442706

HACKING TIMBUKTU

STEPHEN DAVIES

Long ago in the ancient city of Timbuktu, a student pulled off the most daring heist in African history — the theft of 100 million pounds worth of gold. It was never recovered but now a cryptic map of its whereabouts has been discovered.

Danny Temple is a good traceur and a great computer hacker. When the map falls into his hands and he finds himself pursued by a bizarre group calling itself *The Knights of Akonio Dolo*, both of these skills are tested to the limit. From the streets of London to the sands of Timbuktu, this high-tech gold rush does not let up for a moment.

9781842708842